THE
WEEKEND
AWAY

BOOKS BY MIRANDA SMITH

Some Days Are Dark

What I Know

The One Before

Not My Mother

His Loving Wife

The Killer's Family

The Family Home

The School Trip

THE
WEEKEND
AWAY

MIRANDA SMITH

bookouture

Published by Bookouture in 2023

An imprint of Storyfire Ltd.
Carmelite House
50 Victoria Embankment
London EC4Y 0DZ

www.bookouture.com

ISBN: 978-1-83790-518-8
eBook ISBN: 978-1-83790-517-1

For Allison

PROLOGUE

I'm sprinting through the dark forest, branches biting my shoulders, roots snaking around my feet. I fall forward, the landing so powerful it empties what little air is left inside my lungs. My arms reach forward, searching for balance. The soil, grainy and moist, clumps between my fingers.

There's something else down here with me. Something that doesn't belong. I feel the unmistakable texture of skin. A body, motionless, rests beside me in the dark.

Another dead body.

Another life lost.

Because of me.

I jump upward, continuing my climb. With each ragged breath, smoke fills my lungs. The fires are getting closer, coming to consume all the evidence of the sins we committed this weekend.

When I look behind me, I can see the flames getting closer. Ribbons of orange and red, rising from the ground, licking the night sky, devouring the mighty forest.

And yet the fires aren't my only fear.

Someone else is out here in the darkness with me.
Someone who wants me dead.

ONE

SIENNA

The woman in front of me won't stop shouting, but I manage to tune her out, focusing my attention on the stained tablecloth she holds in her hand.

It's going to be a devil to clean. Near impossible. The blemish has bled, spreading into the delicate fibers of the fabric. Clearly, it's been there a while. My guess is it was soiled last Saturday, during one of her fancy dinner parties, and she just now got around to running errands.

"Are you even listening to me?" the woman shouts.

This time, her voice slices through my subconscious, and my eyes lift away from the fabric, back to her. The woman yelling is Mrs. Whitmore. White, middle-aged, creaseless forehead and sunken eyes. She's on the "frequent complainer list" I posted in the back. Ma keeps taking it down, but I tack it up again anyway, a form of silent protest.

Mrs. Whitmore lifts the cloth higher, as though I haven't seen it already. "This is a family heirloom. I'm not going to drop if off here without a guarantee you can restore it."

"I understand, Mrs. Whitmore," I repeat. "But as I've told you already, we can't make any promises. Especially when it comes to red wine stains that have already gone through a wash cycle."

Her peach lips make a perfect circle. "I never said it had gone through the wash."

She didn't need to tell me. I catch a waft of the generic, store-brand detergent, and can see the dull pilling from where she's already tried, in vain, to remove the stain herself.

"You know what, we've been supporting this business for over ten years." She stuffs the tablecloth back into the white garbage bag she brought and huffs. "If it's this much of a hassle, I can take our clothes somewhere else."

I smile, patiently. "We'd sure hate to see you go, Mrs. Whitmore. I'd recommend Donald's Cleaners across town. It's about a twenty-minute drive from here, and there's still no promises they can remove the stain, but they'd be your best bet."

I'm not sure what Mrs. Whitmore was expecting. That I'd break down, tell her what she wanted to hear. Or perhaps whip out some magical potion that could remove an unremovable stain. We lock eyes in a staring duel, and, as usual, the person in the wrong is the first to break.

"Fine." She drops the garbage bag on the counter and starts searching for her wallet inside her leather handbag. "Try your best. I guess that's all you can do. Should I pick it up at the usual time with next week's order?"

"That would be just great, Mrs. Whitmore." I smile. "Thank you so much for your loyal business."

She rolls her eyes, turns on her heels and marches toward the clear-glass doors. The smile on my face doesn't drop. I wait until she's outside before I raise my left hand and give her the bird.

"Sienna?"

Dad calls my name from the back. The waiting room is empty, so I leave the front desk, walking down the narrow hallway which leads to the industrial washing room where the magic happens. My father is in his mid-sixties now. If it were up to him, he'd have retired years ago. Roth Family Cleaners was only supposed to be in business long enough to get my sister and me through college, and yet there always seems to be some reason for them to keep the doors open a few more years.

"Problem?" he asks. He's leaning against a metallic folding table, droplets of sweat sprinkled over his body. It gets increasingly hot back here in the summer, when all the washers are thundering at once and the hot-pressing machine is in constant use. Looking at my father now, I wish more than anything that he could rest.

"Nothing I can't handle. Let's take lunch," I tell him. "I'll lock the front door. We can turn off the machines and give you some time to cool off."

"We're already behind. I'm not going to be able to stop for at least a few more hours."

"They're just clothes, Dad. People will understand—"

"It's not just clothes, Sienna. This is our livelihood. Business is booming ever since the cleaners on Eighth Street closed down. We should be celebrating that."

Business isn't really any better than it was a few years ago. It only feels like more work because his working partner, Ma, isn't capable of helping him the way she once did. I've tried to join him in the back more than once, but he always brushes me off, saying I'm doing enough charity by manning the front.

"Your mother should be in the break room," Dad says, turning his back to me. "If you're hungry, I'm sure she wouldn't mind working the counter for a while."

Before I can make any more suggestions, he's put his headphones back over his ears and returned to hauling loads into the machines. I turn, tracing my steps down the same narrow hallway, pausing at the door on the right and pushing it open.

"Ma?"

She's sitting on the sofa, her feet propped up on the coffee table. The television is loud, one of those paternity court dramas where people yell and cry. I look around the small room for the remote.

"I was thinking of getting lunch," I say. "Do you think you could watch the front for a while? I can bring you something back, if you'd like."

She doesn't answer. The television is so loud, I wonder if she heard me. When I finally mute the volume, and turn to face her, I realize she's asleep. I move closer to the sofa, taking the blanket that's around her legs and raising it to cover her entire body. That's when I catch the whiff of liquor. It's just past noon, and Ma has already checked out for the day.

I exit the break room. Against Dad's orders, I go to the front door and lock it, sliding over a sign that says: *Lunch Break. Be back in twenty.* Both my parents are occupied, and I need a few minutes away from the business, otherwise the next stuck-up customer to stroll through our doors will receive the full brunt of my frustrations.

The autumn weather is breezy and cool compared to the stuffy lobby, heat from the backrooms constantly making its way to the front. Every day, I promise myself I won't go back there. Then I remember that my parents need me. Neither one of them can run the business on their own, and they're both too stubborn to close the doors. We're all stuck, in different ways, and I've learned to accept that.

I cross the street, ignoring the crosswalk several feet ahead. Our hometown is small. There are not very many people out, especially on weekday afternoons. My go-to lunch spot is Brendan's Deli on Main; it's close enough I can get a bargain meal and be back in time to re-open the store before Dad realizes I've skipped out.

I enter the deli. Brendan's layout is similar to Roth Family Cleaners, except there is cooking equipment in the back instead of industrial washers. There are a few small tables scattered in front of the windows. All are empty, except one. A lonely man I've seen walking around town before is sitting at one of the high-tops, nursing a cup of coffee.

At the counter is one other customer. Mrs. Whitmore.

"I'm telling you, Brendan, this town is going to hell. You can't rely on good service anymore."

"I know it," Brendan says. His back is to Mrs. Whitmore and me. He's on the sandwich line, likely preparing whatever meal she ordered. "We've gone through six different servers in the past two months."

"No one wants to work anymore!"

I overhear a rendition of this conversation at least five times a week. There's nothing a sleepy town enjoys more than critiquing capitalism and work ethic. I roll my eyes, contemplating whether I should leave now, before either of them spots me.

"You know, I just left Roth's across the street. They used to be some of the hardest workers in this town," Mrs. Whitmore continues. "Now, it's like they don't even try. I'm going to have to change zip codes if I want proper service anymore!"

I'm about to give Mrs. Whitmore a piece of my mind, but Brendan beats me to it.

"Hey, give the Roths a break. They've had it rough," he says, and part of me wants to reach out and hug him just for saying it.

"Who hasn't had it rough the past couple years?" Mrs. Whitmore says. "That's the problem with this world. People would rather complain and give up than actually put in some hard work."

"I'm talking about their daughter," Brendan says. "The one that died."

The room goes silent, or maybe it only seems that way to me, as the constant truth I try to avoid hangs over me. My sister Samantha is dead. Everyone knows it, and yet I don't believe anyone feels her loss the way I do. I look to the left and catch the man sitting by the window staring at me. He offers a sympathetic look. Even though we don't know one another, he must know of me. I'm the *other* Roth girl.

"I'd completely forgotten," Mrs. Whitmore says, placing a hand on her chest. "How long has it been?"

"A year. Maybe more."

I walk backwards, until I reach the front door. I push it open quietly, aiming to exit the deli without being seen. As I'm leaving, I catch the last part of their conversation.

"Losing a child. How utterly tragic," Mrs. Whitmore says, cocking her head to the side. "It just breaks my heart."

TWO

There's another restaurant about a block away from the cleaners. The food isn't nearly as good as Brendan's, but it's the only place within walking distance. I'm taking the last bite of a savory barbecue sandwich when my phone rings.

I groan in frustration, expecting Dad; I figure he's popped out of the back long enough to see I closed up against his orders. Instead, the name belongs to someone I wasn't expecting to hear from on this dreary Wednesday afternoon: Jackson, one of my late sister's best friends.

My first reaction is to ignore the call, the same way I try to avoid most interactions with people apart from at work, then I think of Samantha. The way Brendan and Mrs. Whitmore were talking about her only moments ago. It'd be nice to hear from someone who remembers Samantha the way I do. The good parts of her life, not just the way it tragically ended.

"My money was on you ignoring my call," Jackson says when I answer. "How ya doing, Sienna?"

"I'm good," I say, wiping my mouth with a napkin. There isn't anything interesting about my life to share with him. Even if there was, I doubt he'd care. Jackson was never really my friend. Just Samantha's. "How are you?"

"Can't complain. Busy with work. Believe it or not, they've finally given me a high-level marketing role."

"Good for you."

Jackson works for Sunshine Aesthetics, the social media marketing company my sister started before her death. Big-ticket influencers and up-and-coming businesses rely on Samantha's company to provide endless content, dreamy creative campaigns, and, most importantly, more followers. I used to joke with her about being on Instagram and TikTok for a living, but her company is all about strategy. People are more likely to buy products off their social media feed than a print advertisement these days, and my sister's company makes it easier for her clients to reach their potential consumers.

When Samantha first met Jackson, he was a well-known partier at Westwood College, the same school she attended. They entered college around the same time, but due to his penchant for partying, he didn't rack up credits at the same rate as Samantha and their other classmates. Anyway, he eventually earned his degree and started working with my sister. There was a whole group of Westwood grads that used to hang out with each other, but I only knew them in passing, through Samantha. Now, they all work together at my sister's company.

"As much as I love compliments, that's not why I'm calling." Until now, I could almost imagine his mega-watt smile as he delivered each line. He pauses, and I sense his laid-back demeanor tensing when he speaks again. "I'm calling about Sammie."

Sammie. I hate hearing people call her that. It makes my sister sound like a dumbed down version of her actual self. A shell of the independent woman she was. Really though, why else would he be calling? Why did he—or any of her friends—spare me any attention, if not for her? The way he talks about her, in the present tense, I can almost imagine she's still around. Like she'll open the doors to the diner, plop down on the booth beside me and berate me for not ordering her any food.

"What about her?"

"It's been almost a year since her death."

"Yeah, I know."

"Of course, you do." He begins talking faster. "I know how hard this year has been on us. I can't even imagine what it has been like for her family. And if you're like me, all of us, I'm sure you've been dreading it."

I have. In one week's time it will officially be an entire year since my sister walked this earth. Even longer since I've seen her.

"And yet you thought I needed a phone call to remind me?"

"No. I'm not trying to remind you." He pauses again. "I'm planning something. We're all planning something, really. A way to remember her. One of our trips. We've rented a cabin in the Smoky Mountains. We're planning a trip this year to honor her. And I wanted to invite you."

I'm familiar with their frequent trips. It used to be one vacation a year. An all-inclusive resort in Mexico or skiing in Aspen or a cabin in the Poconos. Once they started working together at Sunshine Aesthetics, they seemed to travel more under the guise of 'business trips.'

"You want me to join you on your vacation?"

"It's only a weekend. And it's just two hours away from where you live."

"I'm still not sure why you want me to come."

"Because the weekend is about honoring Sammie," he says. "You're her sister. Her twin. I think it's only right that you join us."

"Who all is going?"

"The regular group."

Of course, they refer to themselves that way. Like they're

the cast of *Friends* or something. Just say *the group* and it's immediately clear who is involved. Samantha and Harper knew each other the longest, having become friends back in high school. She met Matilda and Nessa at college. Colby, whom she also met in college, had been her boyfriend for the past eight years. I've been around all of them in some capacity before, because of Samantha, but without her in the mix, I can't think of any logical reason why I should go. Jackson is the only one I can even partially stand.

"I'm not sure," I say to him. "The six of you were always so close. It would probably be nice for you to remember her together, without me."

"We all loved Sammie, that's true. And because of that, we were close enough to know she loved you more than all of us put together." He waits. "It's not right doing anything in her memory and not having you there."

My throat feels raw as I try to swallow down tears. The only way I've survived this past year is by thinking of Samantha as little as possible. Most of the time, I imagine she's busy at the company she started, having the time of her life, that I'll see her again come summer or the holidays. Whenever I remember she's gone forever...

"Sienna, are you there?"

"Yes, I'm still here." I clear my throat. A weekend away to memorialize the death of my sister is too much. Too soon. "I'm not ready for something like that. I'm still... processing."

"I understand." He sighs in defeat. "I at least wanted you to know you're invited. We're not leaving until Friday night, so there's still time for you to change your mind. Think about it, okay?"

My phone beeps with an incoming call. The screen reads *Dad*.

"I appreciate you thinking of me, Jackson," I say. "But I have to go."

"Don't be a stranger?"

I click over to the other line without saying anything else. I can hear the roaring of the washers in the background as my father begins to speak.

"Where the hell are you?"

"On my way back." I'm standing now. "I wanted to get lunch—"

"Your mother is passed out in the break room," he cuts me off. "You were supposed to ask her to work the counter."

I sigh. "I know, but... I thought she could use the rest."

He pauses. There's so much being said in the silence. Ma hasn't been right since Samantha died, but Dad is too much like me. We both ignore what's happening around us, marching on like we always do.

"You're on your way back?"

"Two minutes."

"Okay then."

He hangs up.

A year ago, I never would have thought this would be my life. That I'd spend six afternoons a week working at Roth Family Cleaners. That I'd be juggling the heavy emotions of my parents all by myself. And that my sister would be gone forever.

THREE

When I found out my sister had died, I was in Paris. A German man with bleached-blond hair had his hand up my blouse. We were in the back of some underground club a friend had told me about. The room was dark, the electronic music loud. I could barely tell the difference between the phone buzzing in my pocket and the constant bass vibrations rising from the cement floors.

I silenced the first call, kept kissing the German guy. My routine was to check in with family during the week, but my weekends were jam-packed, and they knew that. When the phone started ringing a second time, I pushed the guy off me and pulled away from the wall.

"*Was?*" he said, wiping his chin.

"Phone," I said, as obnoxiously as I could, pointing at the device in my hand. I left him there, on the bottom floor of the club, absolutely certain we wouldn't cross paths again.

By the time I made it outside, the cool night air tarnished by the smell of smokers lingering around the club's entrance, I was afraid I'd taken too long.

"Ma?"

Strange sounds crackled over the line. I wondered if the call had already dropped, or if I was in one of those bad zone pockets sprinkled around the city.

Then she spoke: "Sienna?"

It was her voice, yet it wasn't. She sounded weak and far away, further away than the actual distance presently between us.

"Ma?"

She exhaled. "You need to come home."

"Ma, it's after midnight here," I said, which meant it was almost six in the morning there. My parents were early risers because of business, but wasn't it Sunday? Their day to sleep in? Besides, they were fully aware I would be abroad for another four months. What was she going on about?

"I don't want to tell you this over the phone," she said, her voice growing stronger.

My stomach dropped then. "What's happened? Is it Dad? Is something wrong?"

A strangled cry escaped her lips, traveled the distant miles through the phone wires, piercing me directly in the heart. "It's your sister. Sammie. She's dead."

Not injured. Not in trouble. Dead. There was an impossibility to what she was saying I couldn't wrap my head around. It felt like everything inside of me—my heart, my stomach—dropped low, to a place yet undiscovered, leaving a vast emptiness.

Samantha couldn't be dead. She'd walked this earth for as long as I had, give or take a couple of minutes. It must be a misunderstanding on my end. It was late. Good luck counting how many drinks I'd had tonight. Music continued to blare, making it hard to listen or think or process any of what was happening around me.

"Sienna, speak to me. We can come to get you if you need. You shouldn't be alone..."

But I'd already begun to tune her out, block out so many parts of the life I'd lived up until that point, the majority spent with my sister by my side.

My sister and I were born in the early hours of a stormy August morning. Over the years, we both grew into the expectations of our alliterative names: Samantha was classic, timeless; I was bolder, more dangerous. Growing up, I was the one to start mischief, and Samantha was the one to get us out of it.

Samantha became the prototype for what every young girl wants to be. She worked hard in school and joined programs that earned her the respect of teachers and peers alike. She was a gifted volleyball player and cheerleader. Member of the homecoming court. I'd like to say I was beside her every step of the way, but the more accurate description would be I cheered her on from afar, usually from the confines of Saturday detention. Ask anyone who knew us, they'd all say the same thing: *Sammie is the golden child, and Sienna, well, there's a misfit in every family, isn't there?*

We were different, but that's what made us great together. Yin and yang. Fire and water. Earth and sky.

Despite our warring temperaments, we couldn't have been closer. Samantha might have been the perfect one, but she somehow became the only person in my life who never made me feel less-than. She praised my rebellious spirit as much as I, and the rest of the world, valued her completeness. My smart, beautiful, popular sister, who always erred on the side of caution, couldn't die at the age of twenty-eight.

Besides, I was the fuck up. The wild card. Moments ago, I'd been necking some stranger in an underground disco, doing my best to sow my wild oats before my parents lowered the hammer on my dreams. Samantha gave me hope that one day I could get it all right. The grades. The grace. The guy. The respect. How can the person who had it all lose everything?

According to my parents, and later on the police, it was all an accident.

The balcony attached to her third-story condo was aesthetically pleasing, but not sound. She'd tumbled over the railing in the early hours of a Sunday morning. The drop couldn't have been more than ten feet. A hard fall might be deadly for an elderly person, or even a small child. But a healthy, young adult? Apparently, she'd hit her head in exactly the right spot. She became unconscious, and by the time she was found several hours later, she'd lost massive amounts of blood. Within hours of being transported to the hospital, she was pronounced dead.

The simplicity of it angered me more than anything. Samantha wasn't clumsy. It was a freak injury, the doctors said. Like when a bullet comes mere millimeters away from nicking an artery, except in this situation, it was the opposite. If she had landed on any other part of her body, she would have walked away unscathed. At worst, with a broken bone. But that's not what happened. My sister died, alone and helpless.

Because the fall happened in the early morning—around three a.m., according to the medical examiner—no one found her until the next morning. At my parents' request, they did an autopsy. Like me, I believe they were searching for something else to blame. What toppled her over the railing? Was she trying to retrieve something when she fell? Was she pushed? Did a small earthquake rattle the ground in the dead of night at the precise moment my sister stepped outside? Anything.

The answer we were given was much less dramatic. My sister had alcohol in her system—0.11, higher than the legal limit to drive a car. My sister, who rarely drank, was somehow so wasted at three in the morning that she fell over her balcony railing. It was the only explanation, the police said. She was alone at the time of the accident; Colby, her live-in boyfriend, was out of town. And when investigators went through her apartment, they found two empty bottles of wine, only one glass. Her death was ruled a drunken accident, the case closing permanently a week later, when my parents cremated her remains.

Grief soon turned into anger. I refused to accept her death, but beyond that, I refused to accept the way she died. Samantha didn't get drunk or fall or make mistakes or—

My thoughts flurried into a dangerous spiral. Those were moves out of my own messy playbook, and the fact I was thousands of miles away from her when it happened only made it worse. Months had passed since the last time I'd seen her. We spoke on the phone, occasionally, but not nearly enough because I was busy abroad. Our last communication wasn't even a conversation—it came in the form of a voice mail she left me the day before her death.

When I tried calling her back, she didn't answer.

Refusing to accept defeat, I kept going over the details of my sister's death. There wasn't much to investigate. Even her body had been reduced to nothing more than the ashes which sat in a decorative urn in our family's dining room. Still, I needed to know more. What had happened to my sister in the hours before she died?

"We could ask for police reports," I told my parents. We were in the lobby of Roth Cleaners, the first day we reopened after the funeral. "There might be something in there that makes sense of what happened. Something the police missed."

"What are you trying to find, Sienna?" Ma asked. That same strange voice I'd heard over the phone in Paris was now a forever part of her, it seemed.

"I don't know," I answered, honestly. "Samantha's death doesn't make sense."

"Death rarely does," Dad said. He sat on the old sofa in the lobby, his head lowered, shoulders raised, as though he could fold into himself and disappear.

"There has to be more," I continued, unmoved. "I know

there weren't security cameras around her complex, but what if someone was there with her? What if she was pushed?"

"You're saying your sister was murdered, now?"

"No." It was what I was saying, but it sounded ridiculous. "Maybe it was still an accident, but I can't shake this feeling we're missing part of the story. Samantha wouldn't have fallen by herself. Why was she even on her balcony at that time of night?"

"She wasn't herself." Mom slammed her own drink on the counter. Even from several feet away, I could smell her breath. We all knew what was inside. "The alcohol killed her. She was drunk."

Ma wandered into the back, closing the break room door behind her. She made no connection between the fact Samantha was drunk when she died, and that she'd been drunk every day since.

Dad looked at me with tired eyes. "Not everything is a conspiracy, Sienna. You must let this go."

"She's my sister," I said, passion tied to the end of each word. "I won't give up on her."

"Then let it go for yourself. And for us." He stood, his shoulders never reaching his full posture. "It doesn't matter what happened that night. Nothing will bring her back."

He left me, alone in the lobby, alone in my convictions. After several more moments of deep thought, I knew they were right. Samantha's death was tragic, hard to understand because a loss of this magnitude never makes sense.

I lost my sister, but Ma and Dad lost their daughter. At some point, I needed to move on, let them be the ones to grieve. They were trying to let go while I was holding onto something I'd never be able to prove, something that may never warrant proving. Accidents happened. They were rare in the crime podcasts I listened to or the suspense books I read or the thriller shows I binged, but in real life, they happened all the time. And as awful and anti-climactic as it was, that's what everyone believed happened to my sister. How could I lay her to rest—her body, memory, soul—without accepting that fact?

My mind kept going back to a phrase Ma used to throw around when we were younger: *God protects children and drunks.*

My sister was no child, and apparently, she wasn't drunk enough for God's mercy, either.

FOUR

As much as I try to keep everything related to Samantha and her death buried down deep, memories inevitably make their way to the surface. She's all I think about for the remainder of my shift at Roth Cleaners, and she's still at the forefront of my mind as I make the short drive home.

To make the cliché complete, I don't only work at the family business. I'm living in my parents' house, too. It started as a way for us to be closer in the wake of Samantha's death, but as Jackson pointed out, it's been a year. It's unclear why I'm still living here other than I have nowhere better to go.

In the past few years, I'd made my living as a freelance photographer. It wasn't an impressive income, but it was enough to provide food and shelter. More importantly, I loved taking pictures, whether they brought in money or not. I figured I was still ahead of my peers in that sense; they might make more money, but I genuinely loved the freedom photography provided and practically got high off the rush when one of my photographs sold.

Problem is, they didn't sell that often, and what profits I did make were spent on my trip to Europe, which was cut short after my sister's death. Now, living with my parents and working at their business is all that keeps me from being jobless and homeless.

When I walk inside the old ranch-style house, Dad is standing at the breakfast bar, spreading bills across the laminate countertops. Another boring, sad day in middle-class suburbia. Little about this scene has changed since my childhood. Back then, I used to dream about getting away from here, exploring the world. Funny how Samantha's death has brought me back to the same place I always longed to escape.

"Would you like pizza for dinner?" he asks once he sees me.

"Sure."

"I'll call Murray's and get the family special," he says. "That's your favorite, right?"

"Yeah." The house is quieter than I remember, even when we're all home. "Where is Ma?"

"Sleeping." He picks up another envelope, tearing it open with his teeth.

I offer a weak smile. Clearly, Dad regrets getting onto me about closing the shop for lunch. That's the only reason he'd offer to get takeout in the middle of the week. That, and he doesn't want to eat alone. It's usual for Ma to go straight to bed after she returns home from work.

I climb the rickety steps leading to the second floor, careful to avoid the collection of family photos on the wall. My mother used to memorialize everything, from kindergarten graduation to sports events to proms and family vacations. In all the pictures, Samantha and I are there together. She's not added anything to the wall since my sister died; she hasn't taken any new pictures in the past year, let alone smiled.

My bedroom is on the left, but I don't make the usual turn. Instead, my eyes land on the room at the end of the hallway. Samantha's room. Believe it or not, I've not stepped foot inside it since I moved back. Ma goes in there throughout the week, far more often than she comes into my room. Even Dad goes in there from time to time.

But I can't. The rest of the house might seem barren and cold, my room included, but Samantha's room is alive with memories. Our entire childhood is held in those four walls. Getting dressed for school formals and dances, admiring our final looks in her floor-length mirror. Late summer nights staying up to watch scary movies on the old flat screen in the corner. Wrapping presents for our parents around the holidays, blocking the door with her papasan chair so they wouldn't see what we'd made. Her room was the eternal life-source of our home, a fact that didn't bother me until she was gone.

And yet now, part of me wants to push open the door, dare myself to go inside. Jackson's phone call, as well-meaning as it might have been, has set off a reaction within me, one that's impossible to ignore. A year without my sister. Twelve whole months without seeing her smile, or her room or her things.

A quick flick of the light switch, and the room is bathed in a warm yellow glow. Everything is how I remember it from high school. Her vanity, cluttered with various makeup brushes and nail polish containers and combs, sits in front of the window, the curtains of which are pulled to the sides. Her closet door is open, mostly bare, although a few random items of clothing dangle on hangers. Her bed is in the center of the room, the floral comforter tucked beneath a mountain of throw pillows. The coverings aren't just made, but freshly washed. Ma doesn't just visit this room; she still washes the sheets, keeps them clean, as though one day Samantha will simply come home. The realization saddens me.

Besides these details that clamor for my attention, it's just a room. Nothing spectacular. If anything, it's an ode to the bright teenager my sister was, not the polished young woman she later became. Still, it's startling, being here around her things. It's like investigating a secret side to my sister, one her other friends and acquaintances knew little about.

The mattress moans as I sit. I lean back, staring at the lone light fixture in the ceiling. The last time I saw her, we were in this room. It was in the spring, before I took off for my trip around Europe. I'd longed for Samantha to come with me, but she had Sunshine Aesthetics and a slew of other responsibilities that needed tending.

"I'm jealous of you," she said.

She sat on the bed beside me, painting my fingernails a black color called Midnight Spell.

"No one would believe that," I said, trying very hard to keep still.

"I am. You're going to be in Europe for the next six months. If you ever come back, that is."

"Of course I'll come back."

"I wouldn't blame you if you stayed."

"You could come with," I said. "The company will still be there in the fall. You can resume your Girl Boss status then."

"I can't," she said, reluctantly. It wasn't the first time I'd asked her to join me, and it wasn't the first time she'd turned me down. "I have things here I need to finish."

"Are you talking about Colby? God forbid, you take time away from your boyfriend."

"Not *just* Colby." She bent down and blew on my nails to dry them faster. "A lot of work goes into starting your own business, let alone keeping it afloat."

"I get it," I said, even though I couldn't fathom what her life was like, running her own business. None of the responsibilities she mentioned were as important to me as they were to her.

"Europe isn't going anywhere either," she said. "We'll plan another trip. Just the two of us."

"I would love that."

"I need you to have the time of your life now, so that when

I'm ready to conquer backpacking, you can show me all the best spots."

I looked away from her. "If you're serious about planning a trip, maybe I should wait."

"No. You need this now."

"Unlike you, I don't have a whole life I'm leaving behind."

"Maybe that's because you have a whole life you're waiting to find."

I'm not sure how she did it, but Samantha was the only person who wasn't constantly comparing my life to hers. She somehow made me feel I was doing exactly what I needed to do, even when that was nothing. She even used the word *jealous*. No one was jealous of me. Especially not Samantha.

"Can I sleep in here tonight?"

"Sure," she said, lowering herself onto the bed. "Don't mind my alarm, though. Colby will be here by sunrise to pick me up."

I slept through her alarm as easily as I slept through my own. When I woke up the next morning, she was already gone. I felt undeniably sad at the thought I wouldn't see my sister for another six months. If only I'd known that morning I'd never see her again.

I'm still staring at the ceiling, trying to remember what my life was like before Samantha's death. Warm tears roll down either side of my face. I turn on my side, staring at my sister's nightstand. There's a lamp, a framed picture of Colby, and a few bottles of nail polish—they could very well be the same ones she used to paint my nails that last night together.

I stand, quickly, as though sudden movement will keep my emotions at bay. I wander over to the window across from her bed, another memory focal point in my mind. We'd sit here reading in the summer when we were kids. As we got older, it was this window I used to sneak out of the house.

"Be careful," Samantha would hiss at me, as I climbed down

the side of the house. She never lectured me but wanted me to be safe.

I pull back the drapes, moist with dust and age. I look down at the driveway below. The window in my bedroom was at the front of the house. I couldn't have climbed out of it without drawing the attention of all our neighbors, which is why I used Samantha's window. How many times did I do that through the years? A dozen? More? Not once did I come close to falling, and I can guarantee there were times when I was heavily intoxicated.

I wonder, which was farther down, this drop or the one from Samantha's balcony? It must be around the same distance. How could a fall from such a seemingly short distance end her life?

Ma and I visited her condo only once after her death. Dad refused to go. Colby had already hired a moving team to take away his belongings. Said he couldn't bear to spend another night there, knowing it was where Samantha had died. He'd kindly offered to box up her belongings, but Ma insisted we do it ourselves. It was an opportunity for her to perform one last act of service for the daughter forever gone.

Samantha was a tidy person, believed an organized space resulted in a successful life. Maybe she was onto something, because her business was certainly successful, and her belongings were shockingly easy to sort through. Most everything was already boxed and labeled, a far cry from the cluttered attic which stored all my parents' stuff.

All we needed to pack up were the personal items she had scattered around the place. Framed pictures of different vacations she'd taken with friends over the years. In the hallway, an eight by ten photograph I'd taken of our family one Christmas. By her bed, a picture of us.

It was one I took not long after I'd received my first camera, when I first decided to dabble in photography as a potential business, not just a hobby. We were sitting in the backyard of our parents' house, baking in the fading summer sun. Light poured around us at exactly the right angle, and I begged her to let me photograph her. She was reluctant at first, but I eventually coaxed her into modeling. Although our features were almost identical, it always seemed easier to capture beauty in Samantha, rather than myself. At the end of our impromptu photoshoot, I snapped a picture of the two of us, sitting under the large oak tree.

I kept that picture of the two of us for myself.

Before leaving her condo, I dared myself to look outside. I stepped out onto the balcony from which she'd fallen and surveyed the area. The gaps between the railings were wider than I'd like, but they were made of solid steel. I peered down at the hard, charcoal-colored concrete beneath. I imagined bones breaking upon impact, blood spilling from the wounds. But she shouldn't have died. It wasn't that much of a fall, was it?

I eye the window off her bedroom with the same suspicion now, thinking of all the times I braved this exit route and emerged on the ground below without a scratch. A wave of vertigo washes over me, and I look away. On my knees, I lean my forehead against the cushioned window seat. Breathe. Think of anything besides Samantha. It's impossible to do when everything connects back to her. Especially everything in this room.

As I'm kneeling down, eye level with the window seat, another memory comes to my mind, one that is light enough to make me smile, banishing the memories of my sister's fall. I grasp the cushion and wiggle it loose. It pops off like a top, and I reach my hand inside.

The broken bench was something Samantha and I made together one summer. To this day, I don't think either of our parents know about it. Inside, we'd hide anything we didn't want them to find. Twigs and rocks from by the creek, love letters from boys. It's been years since either of us put anything in the crevice, or so I thought.

My fingers dangle over something, the material fresh compared to the weathered items in the rest of her room. A red and orange striped journal, the name *Samantha* written across it in sparkly cursive. My sister's diary.

The sight of it makes me laugh. I didn't realize she'd kept a diary. I know I'd quit writing one when I was a teenager, and I assumed she'd stopped too. I grab the journal and flip through the pages, expecting to see stories from high school or even our childhood days.

Instead, the most recent entries are from 2022, the year she died. I smile, thinking of the sentimental side of my sister I so miss. Then, the sadness returns. These pages captured the last few months of my sister's life.

I flip through them. Almost every page is full. At the back, I notice a few pages have been torn out. I rub my thumb over the torn sections, the wavy edges tickling my thumb, then turn back to the beginning, glancing over the first few pages.

She's writing about Colby and Matilda and Nessa and Harper—all the people who will be at the memorial trip this weekend. These were the people Samantha couldn't bear to leave behind, and yet, she left us all anyway.

Longing to feel closer to her, if only for a little while, I return to her bed, lie back on the mattress and begin to read.

FIVE

The next hour passes in a blur. A whirlwind of memories and experiences, all told through my sister's eyes, in her voice. I don't pull my eyes away from the pages of the diary until the bedroom door swings open.

"Sienna?" Dad stands in the doorway. "What are you doing?"

"Nothing." I sit up on the bed, just managing to slide the diary behind a pillow before he sees it.

"Oh, honey." He comes closer, pulling me in for a hug. "I miss her, too."

I hadn't realized it, but I've been crying. Across the room, I take a peek at my splotchy face in the vanity mirror. When I speak, my voice is raw.

"I'm fine. Really. This is the first time I've been in here... around her things... since she died."

"It doesn't get any easier," he says, and for a moment I'm afraid he's going to start crying, too. That's something I can't handle right now. "But we get stronger. Every day. Remember that."

I nod in agreement, even though the last word I'd use to

describe my feelings in this moment is strong. It's more like shock, confusion, anger.

"I'm sorry for getting onto you about closing the shop today," Dad starts up again.

"Don't worry about it," I say. "That's not why I'm crying."

He cups his warm hand on my knee. "Okay. Come down and eat your pizza."

"In just a few," I say. "Let me shower first."

Dad leaves the door open on his way out, a reminder that I shouldn't allow myself to stay here any longer, locked in a vice of emotions. But so much more is running through my head besides the grief over my sister. I wasn't lying when I told him his outburst isn't what led me down this path today, into her room, inside the pages of her journal.

It was Jackson's phone call.

I slide the diary back where I found it, in the broken window seat, at least for now. If it's been here for a year without my parents finding it, they won't go looking for it tonight, and I was the only other person who knew about our shared hiding spot. Besides, I'd know if they'd read it. They'd likely have the same reaction I'm having now.

My parents were the ones who told me to let Samantha's death go, to stop looking for something to blame. The police were convinced her death was accidental because of the alcohol consumption and the fact she was alone at the time of her death.

As far as we know, that is.

The main reason Samantha's death wasn't deemed suspicious is because no one held any grudges against her. She had no enemies. The world became darker without her in it; no one would want her to die. After reading about Samantha's experiences in the last year of her life, I wonder if that last part is true. The people closest to her had secrets, and she detailed each one of them in her diary. Enough to lay out multiple clear and distinct motives.

Quickly, I exit Samantha's room before either of my parents can see me again and cut into the hall bathroom. Once inside, I take a look at myself in the mirror. My face, so similar to Samantha's face, is puffy and red from the tears.

If it were just the secrets her diary unveiled, maybe that wouldn't be enough to convince me there's more to my sister's death, but the diary isn't the only message she left for me to find. I pull out my phone and scroll through my saved voice mails, clicking on the one she left the day before her death.

Sienna. It's me. Look, I really need to talk to you. And I know you're busy and it's late. Hell, I don't even know what time it is over there, but I really need to talk to you. Something happened, and you're the only one I can trust to talk about it. Call me when you get this. Please. I don't care how late it is. I need you. Now.

Her voice was hushed, quick, like she didn't want anyone to hear. Or maybe it just sounded that way because after every other word, there was an audible sniffle. My cool, laid-back sister had been crying.

I tried calling her back. Of course, I did. I'm ashamed to admit, when she didn't answer, I went about my life. Snapped pictures of locals selling artwork by the Seine. Ate a filling dinner of cheese and fresh baguettes. Washed it down with red wine. And ended up at that club with the German guy where I got the phone call.

Samantha was dead, and it was too late for me to reach out, to ever know what she wanted to tell me.

I need you. Now.

Her words have haunted me ever since that day, my guilt and grief creating an impassable barrier in every area of my life.

Back when I was convinced we didn't have the full story about Samantha's death, I let the police listen to the voice mail, but they only pitied me. The officers, like my parents and anyone else who listened, heard an emotional message between sisters. They didn't hear someone in peril.

To be honest, when I first heard the voice mail, I didn't think my sister was in danger, either. But after her mysterious death, I wondered. And even though my parents eventually persuaded me to give up my bone, the passages I've just read have unburied all of it again.

Before putting my phone away, I make a call. It takes several rings, but eventually he answers.

"Sienna? Is that you?" Jackson is practically yelling into the phone, although he doesn't realize it. Jarring electronic music makes it difficult for either of us to hear. Must be nice to be out partying on a Wednesday night.

"When are you going to the cabin?"

"This weekend. We leave Friday."

"I'm coming," I say, before my usual hesitancy can take over. My anger fuels me into action. I need to continue riding that wave throughout the weekend.

"That's... shit. That's great." He sounds neither disappointed nor happy, just genuinely surprised. "I'm a little busy right now. I'll text you tomorrow with the details. Sound good?"

"Yeah. Great."

I end the call, my eyes drifting upward again, to the mirror. Now when I see my reflection, there's something different in my stare. The unsettled emotions inside rising to the surface, altering my features.

What I read in my sister's diary changes everything.

The way I viewed her.

The way I viewed her death.

Most importantly, it brings up questions about what my sister was really going through in the months leading up to her fall. Her journal was the ultimate confidant, the person she whispered secrets to when I was too far away to hear.

And Samantha didn't just write about her own secrets. She chronicled her friends' secrets, too, and there were plenty.

Colby, the boyfriend to whom she'd devoted the last years of her life. Harper, her best friend since middle school. Nessa and Matilda, the ones she befriended in college, who later helped her start her company. Even Jackson had his secrets.

Samantha knew them all, and now I know them, too.

SIX

TROY

Fall is Troy's favorite time of year. People wouldn't expect that of him. Given his age and stature, you'd think he'd prefer summer, when he could sneak away to the Gulf, or even Myrtle Beach, kick off his muddy boots and stick his toes in the sand. Or spring, when the restrictions on turkey hunting were lifted and he could go out with his bow.

But neither of those seasons are really Troy's style. He'd never been into hunting—the only one in his friend group who didn't enjoy it—and he was never a big fan of sand, the way it weaseled its way into every uncomfortable crevice. Winter was enjoyable, but only when he wasn't working. The early mornings became torturous after several weeks of icy rain and snowfall, which always made him grateful for fall days like this, when he could go about his monotonous tasks under warm sunlight, against the beautiful backdrop of changing leaves.

He's been awake since four in the morning, as is his routine on Fridays. That is the usual check-in day for renters coming to the cabins. In the winters, bookings were sporadic at best. Some people wanted to come to the mountains for the weekend, only to be disappointed it wasn't the *White Christmas* snowfalls they'd been envisioning. Others would become agitated when they realized even a light dusting of snow left them cabin-bound for hours; salt trucks and machines weren't built for Smoky Mountain terrain, which meant nature and the slow-rising temperatures had to take their course.

In the fall, however, business is steady and constant. Tourists come ready to hike and raft and kayak—all the things that make their Insta feed look so very cool and interesting. Or whatever it was called. Troy isn't big on social media either.

The change in seasons means he spends every weekend checking on each of his three rental properties, making sure everything is in place for the next week's renters. By now, most renters in the area have turned corporate, allowing hourly workers behind front desks to check-in each resident in a separate cabin that resembles a hotel lobby. Or everything is strictly online via booking sites. Owners send over keycodes the minute the deposit has cleared.

Troy is old school. Got that from his father. Sure, he has a small team that helps him. A maid service ensures that everything is clean and sanitary before the next group arrives, washing sheets and shining floors. He has some maintenance guys he calls whenever there is a bigger problem, a busted pipe or a broken hot tub. Everything else is left to him, and he prefers it that way.

This morning, he checks each cabin, making sure it is up to his standards, fixing anything that isn't. Walking away from each place pleased, he drives down the mountain to have lunch at Gary's Grub, another tradition. Gary has good food and loyal customers. Troy often recommends the place to his renters, although he doubts many of them try it; it isn't picture worthy.

Then he retraces his steps, stopping at each cabin to meet his renters for the week. Cabin One—Mountain Serenity—is the smallest. This week, it is inhabited by a young couple on their honeymoon. They seemed pleased enough with the place, but, understandably, were eager for him to take off. He doubts he'll hear from them the rest of the week.

Cabin Two—Celebration Springs—homes a small family getaway for Fall Break. There are five people staying there—a mother and father, two young kids and a grandmother. He figures they might call him later in the week asking for recommendations of places in town to visit. After a few days in the mountains, young children usually have their fill, so he'll point them in the direction of Dollywood or some of the arcades and putt-putt places on the strip.

The last cabin—Sunset Memories—is located the furthest away from the main road and is the largest. Six bedrooms total. It brings in the most money, but also the biggest liabilities. This is what most people would consider the 'party' cabin, the one high schoolers try to rent for post-prom celebrations or college kids for redneck ragers. Hell, he'd even had grown adults trash the place before. Rent to the wrong group of people, and a one-week stay could rack up thousands in damage. Troy has become pretty good at sniffing out who would be a good tenant and who wouldn't, another thing his father has taught him.

Still, as he waits on Sunset Memories' front porch for the renters to arrive, he grows skeptical. Maybe it is because the renters are already an hour late. Maybe it is because he pulled up their file again, only to see the oldest person listed on the reservation is twenty-nine. Sure, that is the same age as him, but Troy is much more responsible than most people his age. He promises himself that if they arrive looking like a bunch of partiers, he'll dig deep and use that stern, Southern drawl to scare the life out of them. Maybe then he won't be punished by picking used condoms from between sheets and spraying puke off the back deck.

A car engine rumbles in the distance. Troy sits up straighter, watching as the white BMW pulls around the corner. He waits on the porch, watching as three people exit.

The driver is a man. Tall and lanky but dressed expensively, with blond hair that falls over his eyes. Business at the bottom, Shaggy from *Scooby-Doo* at the top. Just looking at him makes Troy want to swipe a hand across his own forehead.

"Hey, are you the owner?" the man calls.

He stands. "Yes. Troy Adams. Are you Jackson?"

"That's me." He turns around, talking to the girls behind him. "This is the right place."

"I thought we'd never find it," says the first girl. She holds a book in one hand, which she slides into the large handbag hanging off her shoulder. She looks smart, if not a bit nerdy. Seeing her gives Troy a little hope that maybe this isn't a partying bunch.

Then, something strange. As the girl walks forward, she stops, freezing in place. She stares up at the cabin, almost like she's seeing a mirage, something that isn't really there.

The second girl exits the car and stands beside her. She is wearing frayed shorts and a shirt that rides up past her belly button. Her blonde hair hangs below her waist. There is more hair on her head than clothes on her body, he thinks. When she gets closer to the cabin, she has the same reaction as the first girl. Standing still, whether from shock or fear, Troy can't be sure.

"So, what do you think?" the man asks, clearly expecting a bigger reaction.

The underdressed girl flashes a mega-watt smile. "This place looks great."

She raises her arm and the two high five. The moment of uncertainty is gone. Even the bookish girl seems more at ease. Troy isn't sure what prompted their startled reaction; mountain living just isn't for some people, he figures.

"Are you waiting on more people to arrive?" he asks, hesitantly.

"Yeah. Sure. The others should be here soon."

He isn't sure what *soon* means with this group, considering the first people to arrive are already well past the original check-in time. He walks back to the porch and grabs his clipboard, flipping through the pages of necessary information.

"Have you all read the rules and regulations online?"

"Yeah. Sure," Jackson says.

Troy takes that as an immediate *No*, so he carries on.

"How many adults will be here?"

"Five," says the bookish girl with glasses.

"Actually six," Jackson corrects her.

"It says five on the application," Troy says.

"We had a last-minute addition."

"Who?" the blonde girl asks.

"Sienna."

The trio's giddy excitement pops like a balloon pricked by a pin, that anxious aura from earlier returning. Clearly, this *Sienna* wasn't an addition the other women were expecting. Troy doesn't pay much attention, though. He is irritated that there are already more people staying than originally listed. His sense that this is nothing more than a party crowd is getting stronger.

"I'll give you a tour of the place—"

"Who invited her?" the blonde girl asks, totally ignoring Troy.

"I did," Jackson says. "It didn't feel right not including her."

Whoever this Sienna girl is, it is causing a stir amongst the group, but Troy doesn't have time for drama. He clears his throat and starts again. "Look, this is a small, family-run business. I don't just rent to anybody, which is why I don't go through Vrbo or any of those other big-name sites."

He turns his attention back to Jackson. For some reason, this guy spikes his suspicions the most. "What brings you out this weekend?"

"We're organizing a memorial for our friend who died."

"Oh."

Troy wasn't expecting that. His stomach clenches at the awkwardness of it all. Everyone's eyes seem suddenly on the ground. Perhaps he misjudged this group. Now he feels guilty for giving them a hard time.

"I'll give you the rundown on the place," he says, walking toward the cabin. "Tell you how to work the hot tub and show you the lockbox in case of emergency."

"Emergency?" The blonde girl laughs. "It's not that deep. We're here to relax."

His stomach flips again. Troy isn't sure what it is about this particular set of renters, but they make him uneasy. Sure, maybe they aren't going to turn his cabin into a kegger for the weekend, but they still have liability written all over them. They are city folk, clearly. Totally unaware of the dangers that could be lurking out in the middle of nowhere.

SEVEN

SIENNA

Everything looks the same. I've been driving in circles for what feels like an hour, trying to follow the shitty directions Jackson sent in his text. He'd offered to drive me to the cabin, but I declined. Staying a weekend with Samantha's best friends would be annoying enough. I wanted my own car in case I needed time to myself.

Now I'm starting to regret that decision. I'm not used to driving on these mountain roads, and the GPS directions are inaccurate. Cell service is weak, too, which means every time I've tried to call Jackson, it goes straight to voice mail. What's the point of having my own car if I can't even find the place? And if I do need to leave, what will I do? It's bad enough to make this trek during the day; I can't imagine trying to navigate these roads at night.

As much as I'm already picturing making a getaway, I need to remember why I'm here. It's to figure out the truth about what happened to Samantha. After reading her journal, I'm convinced there's more to the story of her death, and someone at this cabin can fill in the gaps. There are literal missing pages from the diary—either ripped out by my sister or someone else.

I'm not totally convinced someone meant her harm, but now that I know their secrets, it's clear all her friends had a motive to want her dead.

My parents decided to cremate Samantha; the decorative urn that houses her remains sits on our dining room table. Those were her wishes. If her body did hide any clues about what happened to her, if she was pushed rather than falling, the police will never be able to determine that. If her death was more than an accident, we'll never know.

Unless I can coax a confession out of one of her friends.

I plan on confronting them, one by one, until I uncover the truth.

A small animal with a fluffy tail prances in front of my car, causing me to slam on the brakes. As quickly as it appeared, it's gone. I'm not sure if it was a squirrel, a fox—I feel like I've stepped inside the pages of a children's book. Me, the woods, and my animal friends. I can't even remember the last time I passed a car. Do humans exist this far out in the forest?

Frustrated, I shout, pushing hard on the horn. The sound disturbs several birds hidden in the trees above me. They take off in a flurry, and I duck down, as though they're capable of reaching through the car and plucking me out. I don't belong here. Everything about this trip is wrong, and yet it's something I must do. For Samantha.

I need you. Now.

I'm the only person capable of uncovering the truth.

I drive further up the hill, which I swear I've already seen three times so far. Even though Jackson's directions insist I take a right, I take a left. His text message has sent me in circles until now; I may not have a strong sense of direction, but I haven't passed any other signs of civilization, and these paved roads must lead somewhere. The cabin must be close.

Three minutes later, the trees spread apart more widely,

exposing clear blue sky, and I realize I'm coming into a clearing. That's when I see it. The cabin. Finally, I'm here.

I suppose I was imagining a more rustic setting, like something out of a horror movie, but the cabin is much fancier than that. It looks as though it's only been constructed in recent years. The dark roof and wooden exterior aren't weathered, and the dark metal surrounding the windows gleams in the sunlight. Modern and beautiful architecture. I shouldn't have expected anything less from Samantha's friends.

There are two cars in the driveway. A truck I've never seen before and Jackson's BMW, which looks like it's in desperate need of a wash.

As though they heard my car arriving, four adults walk onto the main porch. The only one to truly greet me is Jackson. He throws his hands in the air, a wide smile on his face. Behind him is a man I've never seen before and two of Samantha's closest friends, Harper and Nessa.

You can do this, I tell myself, not even pretending to believe it. My stomach tightens, a last-minute signal from my body to retreat, although I have already decided that won't happen.

"Have trouble finding the place?" Jackson asks when I join them on the cabin's massive front porch. He doesn't even let me get all the way up the steps before he's wrapping his arms around me.

"A little."

"Glad you're here." He calls to the other side of the porch. "Let's welcome Sienna!"

Harper walks over to me slowly. She looks very much like the girl I remember from high school, but her face is round and plump thanks to a strict regimen of fillers and Botox. She scans me up and down, like I'm a fine jewel she's appraising, trying to determine whether I'm real or a knock off. Compared to Samantha, her real friend, I'm the latter.

"It's been a long time." When she gets close enough, she

pulls me in for a brief, weak hug. Her floral perfume fills my nostrils. "Glad you could make it."

I'm not convinced that's true. Although Jackson is my favorite of Samantha's friends, I've known Harper the longest. We were schoolmates all through middle school and high school. I was never close with her, like Samantha was, but she was still always there, attached to many of my core memories from growing up.

Nessa comes walking up behind her. She doesn't initiate a hug, just a delicate wave. I've only met her a couple times. Nessa was Samantha's roommate when she first arrived in the dorms at Westwood College. She has accompanied her to our house for various holidays and weekend visits, but it's probably been two years since we met.

I take that back. She was at the funeral, but I can't remember the last time I was around her when Samantha was alive.

"Wow. You look so much like her." Nessa smiles. "I mean, obviously. You're twins and all. It just takes me back a little."

I tuck a strand of hair behind my ear, not sure what to say. This isn't the first time I've received this reaction, and it won't be the last. It happened before she died, and more painfully now that she's gone.

Someone behind her clears his throat. It's the man I don't recognize.

"Uh, Sienna, this is..." Jackson says, raising his hand toward the man with his shirt tucked into his jeans, waiting.

"Troy." He looks up and down the length of the porch. "I'm the owner."

"Beautiful cabin," I say, looking at the others. "Don't you think?"

Harper looks at Nessa, while Nessa stares at the forest beyond. Neither of them comments about the house, which makes me wonder if a rustic retreat isn't up to their travel standards.

"I think it's great," Jackson says, oblivious to the others' reactions.

"Where are Matilda and Colby?" I ask.

"They rode together," Jackson says.

It only lasts for a second, but Nessa and Harper share another look.

I can't shake the feeling that, regardless of Jackson's invitation, I'm not welcome here. Harper quickly looks at me and smiles, but it's that same reaction I remember from high school, my sister and her best friend hanging out in the room across the hall. Samantha invited me to join them, but I always got the impression Harper didn't want me around.

I take in the view. It looks as though the porch wraps around the length of the cabin, to what I'm assuming is a spacious deck out back. On the left side of the porch is a two-seater swing dangling in the wind. To my right, a small wooden box with a chain around the handles.

"What's that?" I ask.

"That's the trash box," the owner says. "I was telling your friends here about the safety precautions. This one is important. When you take out trash at the end of the night, you must place it inside the bins and make sure you lock it back."

"Why?" asks Harper, a tinge of annoyance in her voice.

"Because of the bears."

"Bears?" Nessa and Jackson say in unison.

"They get a whiff of leftover food, they come looking to feed, and if bears start sifting through trash, they're likely to come back again. The extra lid helps with the smell." The owner crosses his arms. "I already showed you the storage closet in the basement. Anything you need should be in there."

"Thanks," Nessa says. "I think we're all set."

"Well, do you have any other questions?"

"Believe it or not, this isn't my first time renting a place," Harper says.

The owner smiles, strained. "I just like to make sure everyone has what they need. Usually, people have a ton of questions. About bears and hiking trails. Unless they're just here to party."

"We already told you, that's not what this weekend is about," Jackson says, his voice stern. Did they really tell this stranger we were here on account of my dead sister?

The owner—Troy—looks at me. For several seconds, he stares at my face, searching, then looks away.

"Right. After nightfall, it can seem pretty isolated. If you run into any trouble, my phone number is listed on the fridge. Cell service is kind of iffy this far out. That's why there's a landline in the kitchen." He steps off the front porch, headed in the direction of his truck, before he turns back. "One last thing, if you start a fire outdoors in the pit, make sure you don't leave it unattended. These winds can get strong. One little spark could set the whole woods ablaze."

Harper turns to the man. "Geez, you sure know how to get the party started."

Troy only nods and smiles.

"Come on, Nessa," Harper says. "Let's pick our rooms before the others call dibs."

The two prance off in the direction of the house. Harper bolts through the front door like she can't get away from us fast enough. Nessa, however, pauses, inspecting the entrance closely, almost like she's afraid to walk inside. Eventually, she does, leaving me alone outside with the two men, one I barely know, and the other I don't know at all. That sickening feeling returns, the one that warns me I've made a mistake by coming here.

An engine rumbles in the distance. We all turn in the direction of the treeline, watching as a black SUV, obnoxiously large and shiny, parks behind my old Mustang. Even though the windows are tinted, I know it's Colby. The car is flashy and unnecessary, just like him.

"Finally," Jackson says, relief in his voice. "The main man is here."

The passenger door opens first. A woman jumps out of the seat, long dark hair parted at the center. My breath catches. For a moment, I thought it was my sister. Samantha. Then I realize it's only someone that favors her. Matilda. They have very different features, but from a distance, they could pass as the same person. It must be a smaller reaction to what everyone else feels when they see me.

My breath catches a second time when the girl strides over to the driver's side of the car. The door opens, and Colby steps out. Tall and muscular as ever, like a life-sized Ken doll, wearing a light-blue shirt and khaki shorts. But it's not the sight of my sister's longtime boyfriend that clutches my chest. It's the fact that he bends down and plants a kiss on Matilda's lips.

"What the fu—"

Jackson puts his hands on my shoulders, spins me around. "Sienna, there's something I need to tell you."

I pull back, staring at the couple as they walk toward us. Holding freaking hands. They're still too far away to see us—or at least see me. Or maybe they're just too enveloped with one another to care.

"Are Matilda and Colby—"

I'm interrupted again, this time by Matilda's high-pitched voice. "Jackson, we made it!"

"Hey, guys." Jackson's voice is filled with absolute dread.

The couple freeze when they are close enough to see me. They both stare ahead, their jaws slightly lowered. I wonder if they're genuinely shocked I'm here, or if, like everyone else at first glance, they believe they are seeing a ghost.

"Sienna?" Colby says.

My eyes narrow, pure anger steaming out of every pore of my body. Afraid of what I might say—something that could irrevocably ruin the weekend and what I came here to do—I spin on my heels, stomping the short distance to the cabin.

As I'm walking inside, I hear the owner say, in his deep, Southern twang, "You must be the long-lost Colby."

EIGHT

The frame rattles as I slam the door behind me. Nessa and Harper are sitting on barstools in the kitchen, already digging into a box of Thin Crisps. They pause when they see me, like they've been caught doing something wrong.

"Sienna, are you okay?" Nessa asks.

"Colby and Matilda are here," I say. "Together."

Harper's eyes go wide. "Oh, shit."

"Are they a couple?" I ask the obvious. There must be something I've misinterpreted, something that doesn't make sense. My sister's best friend and her boyfriend can't be sleeping together less than a year after she died.

"Jackson didn't tell you?"

"No. No one told me," I say, raising my arms, before flapping them back down. "I take it both of you already knew."

"Yes," Harper says, hesitantly. "We all work together. It's not a secret."

"How long has it been going on?"

"I'm not sure," Nessa says, her eyes darting over to Harper for backup. "Months."

I scoff, shaking my head. "This is unbelievable. We're supposed to be here to honor Samantha."

"That is why we're here," Harper says. "We promise, that's what all of us wanted to do. Remember her."

"And none of you think it's weird?"

"We did at first. Yeah. But Colby and Mattie have been together for a while now. We've had time to get used to it."

"Someone should have told you," Nessa adds. "I would have, if I had known you were coming."

As I suspected, my arrival was a surprise to both, although there was clearly more meaning to their shared look from earlier. When Jackson mentioned Colby and Matilda were riding together, I never imagined it was because they were romantically involved, but the rest of the group knew better. Based on the kiss I witnessed between Colby and Matilda upon arrival, they weren't expecting me here either. Why would Jackson invite me to this weekend and not tell the others about it?

"Look, you have every right to react however you see fit," Harper says, "but that doesn't change why we're all here. We loved your sister. All of us."

I replay the cold welcome I received. I think of their shocked faces at my presence, an interloper in their tight-knit group. And I remember the secrets Samantha wrote about in her journal. They might claim to love my sister, but I'm not sure if that's true.

"I need a minute," I say, marching down the hallway to my left.

I'm not familiar with the layout, don't even know where I'm storming off to, but I know I don't need to be around any of my sister's friends right now. I look inside the room to my right, a bedroom. Beside it, another room with two beds. The third room proves to be a bathroom, so I dip inside, shutting the door behind me and locking it.

I stare into the mirror.

This time when I see my reflection, every aspect of Samantha is gone. It's all me. She was the kind one, the one willing to give people the benefit of the doubt. I had never much liked my sister's friends before her death. Now that I know the truth about them, the secrets that were written in the pages of Samantha's diary, I like them even less.

They're all pretenders, used to putting on fake smiles for the rest of the world to see. If you were to scroll through their social media profiles, which I did shortly before embarking on this trip, you'd see nothing but carefully curated façades. Fancy trips and mouth-watering food, all purchased with the swipe of Sunshine Aesthetics' company credit card, a business my sister founded.

You'll see perfectly poised group shots, the five of them, sometimes with others along the periphery, drinking and smiling and laughing. You don't see a group of grieving friends; you see thriving Gen Z-ers, living their best life for the cameras.

The way they present themselves to the world is the way they present themselves to me. It's a fabrication, all of it. Thanks to Samantha's diary, I know the ugly truth each one of them has to hide. Could one of their secrets be big enough to kill for? As much as the diary provides answers, there are still mysteries. Mainly, what happened to my sister in the days before she died. I don't have those answers, because the last few pages were ripped from the journal. Did she rip them out? Or was it someone else? Why would someone take out part of my sister's journal, but leave the rest for me to find? How did it end up in Samantha's bedroom to begin with? All these questions roll around my head, but I focus on what I do know: that her dear friends are not who they claim to be.

They've been going about life their way for too long, putting on masks, each of them willing to acknowledge the others' disguise, to keep their own firmly in place. They hide the reality of their situations from others; worse, they hide it from themselves. It's a way of life they succumbed to long ago.

Before this trip is over, I'll need to go about things my way. I'll confront each one of them with their secrets, until I decide which one of them was set on hurting my sister. I need to know the truth, not just because Samantha deserves justice, but because this gnawing feeling coursing throughout my body won't go away until I get the answers I came here to find.

The need for revenge is all-consuming. Like fire, it can't be contained. One little spark binds with another and another, until there's an entire wildfire. Hot and suffocating and so, so dark, that when you hold out your hand in front of your body, you can no longer see yourself.

NINE

After another few minutes of deep breathing, I swing open the bathroom door.

My breath stalls in my throat when I see a figure standing there.

"Are you okay?" Jackson asks.

I raise a hand to my chest, feel my heart pounding beneath the flesh. "You scared the shit out of me."

"I'm talking about Colby and Mattie," he says, straight to business. "Are you okay?"

I whip my head to the left, looking to see if there is anyone within earshot. The hallway appears empty, but there are too many people here. Anyone could be waiting around the corner, leaning over the banister, listening to our conversation.

Grabbing the collar of his shirt, I pull Jackson into the bathroom and shut the door.

"How long have they been together?"

"Six months," he says, sitting on the side of the bathtub, resting his elbows on his knees. "Give or take."

"And you didn't think you should give me some kind of warning?"

"In my defense, I didn't think you'd even come. You weren't exactly thrilled about the invitation."

That was before the diary, I think. Before I realized here, among this group of people, might be the only place where I can find answers.

"You said this weekend was about Sammie. About honoring her."

"It is!"

"And none of you think it's strange that Colby and Matilda are dating? Seriously, by the looks of it."

Jackson stares at the gray slate floors beneath our feet. He sighs.

"Yes," he says, at last. "I think it's very strange."

For whatever reason, that wasn't the response I was expecting. My body had been gearing up to fire off rebuttal after rebuttal. Now, I'm deflated, watching Jackson as he continues to talk.

"To be honest, a lot of things have seemed strange in the past year. At first, I thought maybe I was losing it. That my grief was making me crazy. There's just this weirdness I can't shake." His fingers expand, as if holding an invisible ball. He gives both hands a stir before clenching them into fists. "Something about Sammie's death isn't right. And I can't talk to any of them about it."

"What do you mean, 'isn't right'?"

"It's hard to put into words." He laughs but sounds sad more than anything. "I think the rest of them know something about Sammie I don't. Something they're not telling me. That's the real reason I wanted you here this weekend. To see if you feel it, too."

I'm so used to being outside of Samantha and her perfect life and her friendships. I'm used to living life on the fringes, feeling like the only one to live in my own experience. What Jackson is telling me is that the paranoia I've been feeling since reading my sister's diary is justified.

"Who do you think is hiding something?"

"I don't know. All of them. None of them." He raises his hands then lets them fall to his sides as he stands.

I wonder if I should tell him about the diary. After all, it's the only leverage I have over any of the people here. I'd planned on confronting each of them before the weekend was over, but is it too soon? Jackson seems sincere, but I know he had a motive, just like all the others. I decide to put him to the test.

"Is there anything you're not telling me? About Samantha?" I ask, testing him. The way he responds to this question will determine whether I can believe him moving forward.

"What do you mean?" he asks, bewildered. "She was one of my best friends."

"Is that all?"

Jackson's jaw clenches and he looks away from me. "There wasn't anything romantic between us, if that's what you're asking."

A while back, when I was reading a true crime book, I read that sometimes the best interrogation tactic is to remain quiet. People are uncomfortable with silence. Stretch it out too long and they feel the need to fill it, sometimes with a confession.

I use this method now, remaining silent, waiting for Jackson to speak.

TEN

January 2022

Happy New Year!

More like, Cringey, Awkward New Year. Oh, where to even begin?

It happened last night.

Jackson told me he has feelings for me. Yes, Jackson. The one I met at my first kegger at Westwood. I've seen him puke himself more times than I have fingers on my hands. And, of course, he's Colby's best friend.

Yes, that Jackson.

Part of me had wondered for a while if there was something more between us. Jackson flirts, but he does that with everyone. I hear the way girls talk about him. They think he's cute, charming and conceited. We've been friends long enough now; I know that's a front. He leads with his outlandishness because he's afraid people won't stick around otherwise, and he'd rather be the first one to walk away than get left behind.

Either way, back to last night.

It was New Year's Eve. As usual, we headed downtown for dinner and drinks. Colby had more to drink than usual. After the ball dropped, he went over to Nessa's for more partying. I told him I had no intention of going. As of late, all my waking hours are devoted to the business, and I need every moment of shut-eye available. Around four in the morning, I got a call from Jackson, saying that Colby was at Nessa's and too smashed to drive.

I drove over. Jackson had underestimated their condition, especially Colby's. It took both of us to haul him out of the car and up the stairs. Once inside, Colby picked a fight. His typical, drunk routine. He said something about the fact I'd rather be under the covers in my pajamas than go out and have fun with him. I suppose there is some truth in that.

After he fell asleep, Jackson thanked me for giving them a ride, said he couldn't believe Colby wasn't more grateful that I'd left the comfort of my bed to fetch him.

"It's just the booze talking," I told him. "No worries."

Colby doesn't always treat me right, I know that, but I've learned to deal with it. Life's easier when I don't engage in every battle. Tomorrow morning, he'll wake up hungover and hungry. Probably won't even remember our squabble.

Anyway, I got Jackson settled with blankets and pillows on the couch, expecting him to nod off, but he kept talking. Insisting that the way Colby treats me isn't right, that I deserve better.

Part of me has always wondered if Jackson wanted more from me than friendship. The way we hold eye contact a second longer than normal. The way he'd always be the first to jump up and help me when I needed it. Times, like tonight, when he'd be the only person willing to put Colby in his place.

Then, part of me wondered if it wasn't just Jackson being Jackson. Never afraid to be in the minority. He reminds me a lot of my sister, in that way.

Then, he broke down and told me. For more than a year, he'd been trying to fight off his feelings for me. We'd been spending more and more time together since he started working at the company. He said he kept thinking about what the two of us would be like together. Sure, part of it was the alcohol talking, but as I listened, I realized he was also unleashing a deep, hidden truth.

What surprised me wasn't what he said, per se. I'd already had my suspicions. The most surprising part was that I wasn't immediately against the idea. Consciously, I've always considered Jackson nothing but a friend. But listening to him talk last night... the sincerity in his voice... there were moments that felt like I wanted a relationship as much as he did.

Then I thought of Colby sleeping in the next room. Jackson was our mutual friend. Given the dynamics, it couldn't have been easy for him to divulge his feelings; he was only being honest. But acting on my momentary feelings toward Jackson would be a betrayal to Colby and the relationship we'd built. Eight years. Sure, it wasn't always perfect. *He* wasn't always perfect, but I would remain loyal to him.

So, I told Jackson I didn't feel the same way. That I wanted him in my life, but only as a friend. I let him down as gently as possible while also being clear there was no chance of a relationship between us; I didn't want this to become a pattern that would repeat itself in drunken moments. I told myself it was only the alcohol talking, messing with our feelings.

Then I remembered I was sober... Some of what I was feeling must have been real. Right?

The next morning, as expected, Colby woke up and ordered breakfast, and didn't even remember our argument. When Jackson woke, he didn't mention our conversation either. The three of us sat around the dinner table eating biscuits and hash browns, and I'd like to think that whatever came overflowing last night was now bottled up again, under lock and key.

I'm determined not to let one honest conversation ruin the friendship we have, or the relationship I've built. Jackson will always be one of my closest friends.

Lately, I'm beginning to wonder if he's my only friend left.

ELEVEN

SIENNA

The lines written in Samantha's diary replay through my mind as I stare at Jackson, waiting for his response.

"Nothing romantic ever happened between us," he repeats. "But I did have feelings for her."

"Did she know how you felt?"

"Uh, yeah. I told her one night. Several months before she died."

"What did she say?"

Even though I already know the answers to the questions I'm asking, I keep playing dumb. I need to know if he'll answer honestly so I can decide whether to trust him.

Jackson smiles, mischievously. "She turned me down. I should have known better, coming onto my friend's girl. Not to mention my boss. She's too good to do that sort of thing. I think all she ever wanted from me was friendship, and I was fine with that, if it meant she was still in my life."

"Do the others know—"

"No. I'd never tell them," he cuts me off. "I mean, obviously my ego would be hurt. I'm not usually turned down, you know? But I don't think any of them would understand how I felt. It wasn't just that Samantha was smart and funny and beautiful. She was a good person. My feelings were so much deeper than having a crush or wanting to sleep with her. I have a respect for her I've never had for any of the other girls in my life. *Had* a respect."

"That's why her death has been so hard on you."

"Sammie didn't deserve to die young. She deserved a nice, long life surrounded by people who loved her." He pauses. "Who knows, maybe there was a part of me that thought we might end up together. Clearly, Sammie never saw that as an option."

I'm tempted to tell him that my sister did reciprocate his feelings, at least a little, but I'm not sure what good that will do now. And I'm not sure if I should tell him about the diary. Everything he's said until now seems genuine, but I must be certain.

"You had feelings for Samantha, but she stayed loyal to Colby," I say. "You must have issues with the fact he moved on so quickly. With Matilda, no less."

"I am. I mean, it never made sense to me. Colby and Mattie? And how do you move on from someone you spent years with in a matter of months? It wasn't just a breakup either. Sammie died." His voice, once stern, seems to falter, like even he doesn't know what to think. "But they both swear the relationship didn't start until after she died."

"Do you believe them?"

"I don't have a reason not to believe them." He shakes his head. "Truth is, I spent some time away from everyone after it happened. I needed to process my feelings on my own before I could really re-enter the group. By the time I started meeting up for after-work drinks again, Colby and Mattie were an item. It still could have happened the way they said it did, but if there's anything unsaintly about their relationship, the others aren't going to tell me."

"Why not?"

"Because they know I'd confront the both of them." For several seconds, his light-blue eyes are locked on mine, then he looks away, quickly. "Anyway, maybe that's why I've felt like an outsider these past few months. Maybe Harper and Nessa do know something they're not telling me about when it all started. It could be just that, but I can't shake the feeling it's something more."

Out of all of Samantha's friends, I've always gravitated toward Jackson. As Sammie wrote in her diary, he gives off a cocky energy, but I'm able to see beyond that. He's genuine and sincere when he wants to be. Especially about anything involving my sister. I believe I can trust him.

"I agree with you," I say, looking down. "I think they're hiding something, too."

"What do you mean?"

"When you called me earlier in the week, I thought there was no way I'd join you on this trip," I say. "But then I found Samantha's diary. I read it. She revealed a lot of secrets in there about your friend group. I'm wondering if one of the secrets was big enough to make them want to harm her."

With a sudden burst of energy, he hops onto the sink, his arms crossed over his chest. "What secrets?"

"I don't want to get into it yet," I say. "But that's why I came. I wanted to confront all of them. See what they say."

"I took some time away from the group after she died, but I've spent plenty of time with them since. All of them seem genuinely upset about Sammie's death."

"You said yourself, something has felt off. Maybe this is it. One of them might be hiding something, and what's written in that diary might hold the key. I'll tell you what she wrote, but I want to confront each of them first."

He nods. "Okay, so let's go. No point in drawing this out."

"Wait. I mean, we just got here. And I made a fool of myself reacting to Colby and Matilda the way I did. I want to go about this their way, at least at first. Talk to each of them, see what they have to say before they know I'm aware of all their dirty secrets."

Jackson nods. "Okay, and then what? You think one of them is just going to break down and confess to harming Sammie?"

"No. But I'm good at reading people. Samantha used to always say that."

"Yeah, she did," he says. "She really loved you, Sienna."

My throat feels raw, but I push past that emotion, focusing on the task before me, a task for which it appears I now have at least one accomplice. "I don't know how long it will take, but when the time is right, I'll challenge them with their secrets. If one of them did something to my sister, I'll put it together."

"I'm here to help you however you need. I knew it wouldn't be right to come here without you. Between the two of us, maybe we can finally get some answers."

The fact that Jackson and I both have questions about Samantha's death gives me hope that I'm not being paranoid or overreacting. If we arrived at these questions separately, maybe we can reach a conclusion together.

Jackson stands and goes to the door. He turns the knob, then stops.

"In her diary, did she say anything about me?"

Again, I consider telling him, but what's the point? He's earned my trust and telling him that my sister did care for him will only hurt him now, give him a glimpse into a future that never was and will never be.

"No," I say.

"Figures," he says, turning back to the door.

TWELVE

TROY

The woods are different right before dusk. Beautiful. Calm. Deceiving.

Troy descends the mountain in his truck, happy to remain in the valley for the rest of the weekend. He might be the owner of three luxury cabins, but that is just his business. Not as lucrative as some thought, but better off than most expected.

When it comes to his own environment, Troy lives humbly. He inherited a small lot of land by Miller's Creek and bought a cozy double-wide trailer to go there. It isn't quite a home, but it is better than some of the bachelor pads his friends have. Troy keeps the place clean and tidy. There aren't nice curtains or pillows—no sign of a woman's touch—but there are a few family pictures propped on coffee tables and nightstands.

As Troy pulls onto the lot, he hears his dogs barking out back, probably the closest he'll ever get to hearing, *Honey, I'm home.* Twister and Jennings, both bloodhounds, although neither of the animals have been hunting a day in their lives and would probably run scared if they wandered past a bear or a mountain lion.

He exits the truck and grabs a bag of dog food from the

covered porch steps. He pours a serving into each of their bowls, and the dogs whimper gratefully.

Instead of walking inside, he takes a seat on one of the rocking chairs on his porch. The sky is beginning to change colors, large brushes of orange slashing against the light blue, as though the sun has been sliced open, letting its insides spill out. He rocks back and forth on his heels, staring at the beautiful scenery, listening to the pattering of his dogs in the distance.

Troy is happy. Complete. He hasn't felt this way in a long time. Years.

The dogs bark louder, running to the far side of the fence. Probably another woodland animal, daring to get close. The sky is now deep navy, all traces of gold and bronze evaporated.

His mind wanders away, back to the people who had rented his cabins for the week. The small family is probably sitting on the back porch having dinner right about now. He wonders if the father has cooked burgers or hot dogs—always an easy meal for the first night of vacation. The honeymooners are likely keeping themselves entertained, probably won't even leave the cabin for most of the week, unless they take the small trail leading down to the creek. A real pretty spot for pictures.

Although he tries his best, he can't stop thinking of the group staying at Sunset Memories. There is something off about them, and he can't decide why. It isn't just because the house guests showed up late. Sure, he prefers it when everyone arrives together, but that isn't always realistic, especially when people are traveling from different locations.

And it isn't their total ignorance when it comes to the rules and protocols he so clearly laid out for them. Lots of city folk are ignorant when it comes to the woods. If their situations were reversed, he wouldn't appear any wiser. He knows he'd look like a bumbling fool trying to navigate the subway system or hail a cab.

There is something else that bothers him, something he

can't put his finger on. Maybe it is the way they'd interacted with each other. Excited and miserable to be there all at once. Everyone acted on edge when that couple arrived. And none of them seemed particularly happy to have the other girl there either. The one dressed in all black.

Sienna. He remembers her name because he's never heard it before. It is different. And there is something else about her, too. She looks familiar, like he's seen her before, although he knew he'd never rented to a Jackson Pruitt. He'd remember a preppy name like that.

He guesses city folk all start to look the same after a while, just like the people around here wearing nothing but Carhartt and Wrangler.

Normally, when he leaves a group behind for the week, his biggest fear is that they will cause damage to his property. Jackson said they were there for a memorial, so he shouldn't be worried about that. But there is still something...

THIRTEEN

SIENNA

Jackson exits the bathroom first. He cuts left, heading back in the direction of the living room. I go the opposite way, wanting to hide out in my bedroom, when it dawns on me I still don't know which room is mine. My belongings are still outside, sitting on the front porch. I take a deep breath, then walk through the kitchen and living room.

The front door is open. There is a line of white rocking chairs sitting on the porch, each one taken by one of the members of the group. Nessa sits closest to the door, Harper beside her. Colby and Matilda are cuddled up together on the porch swing. When I step outside, everyone halts, as though the very air around us has changed on account of me.

"Sienna, I'm happy you're here." Colby is the first to speak. He stands, the swing wobbling awkwardly. "Can we talk?"

"I just came to get my things," I say, bending to grab my bags. "I don't know which room is mine, but I need to lie down."

Nessa stands. "Here, let me help you. I'll show you your room."

I walk back inside without looking at the others. I imagine

them breaking into gossip the moment I move far enough away. One... Two... Three.

"We thought you might prefer this room," Nessa says.

She stops at the end of the hallway and opens the door on the left. She flicks on the light and steps to the side. The bottom half of the wall has wooden panels. The top half is covered in forest green paint. A large bed, again made of wood, thick, honey-colored trunks, is in the center of the room. There's a masculine vibe. I wonder why they've given this room to me, not Colby or Jackson. Then I remember it's the farthest away from the center of the house. The farthest away from them.

"I don't care where I sleep," I say. "I know none of you want me here anyway."

"We didn't know you were coming," Nessa says. "That doesn't mean we don't want you here."

"Have you gone on any trips together since she died?"

Nessa's face drops slightly. "This is the first. It's been a hard year for the business. For all of us. I can't imagine what it's been like for your family."

I'm tempted to tell her the truth. That Dad ignores Samantha's death by keeping his head down and working, while Ma drinks and checks out completely, but it doesn't seem right to gossip about my parents with Nessa and the others. They might be my sister's friends, but they're practically strangers to me.

"It's been tough. Jackson said that's why he invited me. He wanted me to be included."

"It was the right call," she says, genuinely. "Like Colby said, we're all happy you are here."

Colby. Hearing his name, the first image that springs to mind is him holding hands with Matilda. A hot flash of heat pulses through me.

"I find it hard to believe he's thrilled," I say. "I haven't even heard from him since the funeral. Then I come here and find out he's dating one of her best friends."

Nessa sighs. "I wasn't exactly thrilled when I found out they were together either."

I walk closer to the bed and sit on it. I stare ahead at Nessa, waiting, hoping my silent interrogation technique will do the trick.

"I mean, it was just jarring at first. Sammie and Colby were always together. Back at school, even around the office. Seeing him with any girl would have made me do a double take, but especially Mattie—"

"Why does everyone keep calling her that?" I interrupt. "Her name is Matilda."

Nessa shrugs her shoulders. "That's her nickname."

"Since when?"

"I don't know. The past couple of years?"

Whenever Samantha talked about her friends, it was always Matilda. Then again, there's a closeness that exists within this group from which I'm far removed. Everything Samantha told me was a second-hand account. Even what was written in the diary has her spin on it.

"Anyway, it was hard for me to understand it at first. But Sammie's death affected us all in different ways," she says. "If they found it easier to move on together than apart, maybe that's what works for them."

"When did they start dating?" I ask plainly.

"After Sammie died, if that's what you're getting at."

Nessa is smart. She graduated at the top of her class and is the brains behind Sunshine Aesthetics. But she has emotional intelligence, too. I think she understands the heartache I'm experiencing, perhaps more acutely than even Jackson does. And she understands my biggest fear is that something unto-ward was happening behind my sister's back in the weeks before she died.

"Like I said, I was angry too when I first found out," she

says. "That's the thing none of us want to face. We can be mad all we want. It won't bring Sammie back."

Nessa is right. It doesn't matter how angry I am. How betrayed I feel. My sister is gone forever. I couldn't have expected Colby to be alone for the rest of his life. And Samantha and Matilda were friends; it makes sense that they'd have common traits, similar taste in men. It's just difficult seeing the proof that everyone's life has moved on in the past year. All except my sister's. And mine.

"It's hard without her. Seeing how everyone's life continues but hers."

"I know," Nessa says. "That's how I feel at work every day."

"How is the business going?" I ask.

Sunshine Aesthetics turned a major profit in the two years preceding my sister's death. Samantha and Nessa maintained equal ownership, but after her passing, several shares were up for grabs. My parents received a small payout, as stated in her will, but it was minimal compared to the amount of money the company was worth. A few weeks after her death, the business was bought by the Balding Group, a much wealthier and influential parent company.

"We started the company together. Everyone thinks I'm the brains behind the operation, but it was Sammie's idea. We never would have gotten it off the ground if it weren't for her." She smiles but only for a moment. "It's not much fun seeing what we've created and knowing she isn't here to witness it."

"I know Samantha was stressed about work before she died," I say, focusing intently on Nessa's reaction. "Do you know what was bothering her?"

"Work is always stressful. Putting out fires is always hard," she says, "but it's nothing we couldn't manage together."

As quickly as that light entered her eyes, it's gone. I'm back to seeing the Nessa she puts on for the rest of the world, the person she feels she must be.

"Anyway, can I get you anything else? Harper and I were about to start dinner, but it's been a longer drive for you. Maybe you want something to eat?"

"I'm fine, thanks."

"It's good you're here," she says, before shutting the door.

I always maintain that I don't like Samantha's friends. Maybe that's not wholly true. When it comes to Nessa, I simply don't know her very well. We just had our longest conversation. But she is kind, smart, and driven. Those are the characteristics that attracted Samantha, made her want to start a business with her.

Then I remember the secrets that were written in the journal. As likable as she may be, I know Nessa is lying, at least when it comes to the state of the business before Samantha died. If she would lie to me about that, what else would she try to conceal?

I pull my navy duffel bag onto the bed and unzip it. At the front, sitting atop the piles of unfolded clothes, are two things: a picture frame and the journal.

It's only two nights away; I'm not sure why I brought either of these items. Perhaps I want to feel like she's here with me, even though that's impossible. Seeing the picture of us, scanning her words, makes me feel like she's still around.

And maybe there is another reason I brought the journal. When the time comes for me to confront my sister's friends, I don't want anyone to claim I'm a liar. I'll show them, if I must. Let them know that I have proof, if I believe anyone was capable of doing my sister harm.

Until then, I'll keep the journal hidden, just for me.

I thumb through the pages, rereading what Sammie had to say about Nessa.

FOURTEEN

SAMANTHA'S DIARY

March 2022

I never thought I'd say this, but Nessa is going to be the death of this business.

I know, I can't believe I'm saying it either. Nessa, her high school's valedictorian. Nessa, who could have had any opportunity post-college, yet decided to turn down all those options to start a business with me.

Tax season is always stressful, but even more so when you're trying to get a new business up and running. The team at Sunshine Aesthetics is rounding out, everyone's roles well-defined, but I decided we needed some professional help for tax season. I contacted one of my old sorority sisters, sending over all the necessary financial documents, thinking that would be one less stone on my back.

She's the one who brought it to my attention.

There was one account that wasn't lining up with our profits. I didn't think anything about it at first. Mistakes happen. That's why I'd hired a professional in the first place.

But it wasn't my account. It was Nessa's. I asked her about it, expecting an easy answer.

And she burst into tears.

Nessa has been one of my closest friends for almost a decade. I understand her in ways others don't. She's always trying to prove herself to them, but she doesn't have to be that way with me. That's what makes our bond special, from the first time we bunked up in the narrow dorm room at college.

"You were never supposed to know about this," she said between sobs.

"Know about what?"

"I took some money out of the business account."

"What?" Hearing that sentence spoken by level-headed, responsible Nessa didn't compute. "Why?"

"Because we were stalling. Remember last spring, we were struggling to fund our marketing campaign?"

"Yeah."

"And after we finalized the campaign, business started booming again."

"Right. There's always an ebb and flow."

"Well, I took money from one of our client's accounts so we could pay."

"Nessa!" Rarely had I ever experienced such shock, from Nessa of all people. My mouth hung open, my chest pained. "That's stealing."

"It was only borrowing," she said, quickly. "I've already returned the money I took."

"You said you used personal funds for marketing," I say.

"I didn't have enough," she says. "We had to let our clients and competitors know we were making profits, and putting more money into the company was the only way to do that."

"We were making a profit!" I say. "You didn't have to take money from our clients."

"But not fast enough. You know as well as I do how

temperamental this business can be. Six months is a lifetime, and once people decide Sunshine Aesthetics is old news, that will be the end of us."

"Our popularity is building. We didn't need to move funds around to stay ahead."

"It was one account. The client never even knew it was missing. I've already paid back what was taken. Every cent."

"That's not the point! What if the marketing plan had flunked? We would have been out of that money. We can't earn a reputation for stealing from our clients," I said. "I'm trying to build an honest company."

"*We're* trying to build a company. We started this together, remember? We're the founders. Our say should mean more than the rest of the team."

"What's that mean?"

"Every major deal is run by Colby. Every major investor is wooed by Jackson. Mattie and Harper have their faces plastered all over our social media feeds. I just wanted to feel like I was doing my part for the company I helped create."

"I never thought you'd do something unethical."

On second thought, I should have known better.

I never told the others, but Nessa cheated her way through school. She exaggerated stories to obtain scholarships, even plagiarized part of the thesis which earned her a prestigious post-graduate grant. I found out about that in the same way I learned about this... by stumbling upon meaningless paperwork and piecing it together.

Nessa isn't some criminal mastermind. She said some of her mentors encouraged her to do it, and I believed her. I also believed she wouldn't keep doing it after graduation.

I never told anyone about those incidents. They'd think I was crazy to start a business with someone who lied and cheated, but I never saw Nessa that way. Nessa is brilliant. That's why she was the first person that came to mind when I started Sunshine Aesthetics. Getting through school is one thing. I never dreamed she'd risk losing our business.

"You might think it's unethical," she said. "I call it strategic."

"Don't be strategic like this again. Not when my name is attached to the business."

"I'm sorry. I was desperate and nothing came of it, right?"

"What am I supposed to tell the accountant?"

"That it was a paperwork mistake. It should stay between us. Did you tell the others?"

"No. You're my partner. I came to you."

"Good. Look, every successful company hits a few bumps before they make it to their peak."

And while she may be right in theory, it still didn't sit right when the situation applied to me and my business. I walked away with knots in my stomach. The knots are returning as I recall the conversation now. Even if Nessa made a massive mistake, I don't believe she's a bad person.

I just think she's the type of person who is unpredictable when her back is pushed against a wall.

FIFTEEN

SIENNA

I lift the stiff, bulky mattress, sliding the journal between it and the box spring. It's important to keep Samantha's words safe until the time comes for me to use them.

Her words remind me that the people here are only showing me one side of themselves, the most flattering side. Based on the short conversation with Nessa this afternoon, I'd never guess she's capable of cheating and stealing. That's what makes Samantha's diary such an amazing gift; it gives me details about each of my sister's friends they'd never willingly share.

I've been here less than an hour, and already I feel drained. As tempting as it is to remain here in my room, removed from those I dislike and mistrust, I won't find any answers here. I must join the others if I want to find out what happened to my sister.

Directly across from where I sit, there's a sliding glass door; Nessa was staring out of it earlier. I walk to it, pulling on the handle connected to the pane. There's a small balcony overlooking the side of the house, only big enough for a single chair and table. It would be the perfect place for coffee in the morning, but I'm not a big coffee drinker.

Below the balcony is a small space of grass. A hammock hovers above, tied to two large trees nearby, pillars leading to the wilderness beyond. The forest seems endless—tall, dark trees spreading as far as the eye can see. Looming above them, lush green mountains. At least, I imagine they're green. In the approaching nightfall, they appear navy and gray, craggy lumps enclosing everything.

Movement along the treeline captures my attention. I hear footsteps crunch against fallen leaves, and then I see them. Colby and Matilda, holding hands. Hot, pulsing anger courses through me. I clench the rod-iron back of the chair, finding my balance. The last thing I want to witness is another lover's embrace between the two.

As though sensing my anger from across the way, they drop hands, but don't raise their heads. They don't know I'm here. Their gazes are focused entirely on each other. They're in deep conversation. Although they are only a few feet below me, I can't hear what is being said, but this isn't a casual conversation. Matilda listens intently as Colby becomes increasingly animated, raising his hands and shaking his head. His volume raises, loud enough that a few birds in the closest trees flutter away, carrying enough that I can almost make out what he's saying.

Moments ago, I was overcome with anger. That has been replaced with curiosity. Concern, even. When I see Colby reach out his hand and grab Matilda's arm—

"Hey, did you go for a hike?"

The voice comes from directly below me. It's Jackson. A few seconds later, he appears in the clearing, walking closer to the couple.

Colby drops his hand, and they both smile, looking as carefree as they did when they arrived. It's jarring how quickly their demeanor shifts. What were they talking about only moments ago? What made Colby so angry? Now that

Jackson has joined them, it's like that conversation never happened.

I wander back into the house and exit my room. Down the hallway, I hear muffled laughter. It sounds like Harper and Nessa are in the kitchen, likely cooking dinner.

When I first entered the house, I was so frustrated, I didn't take in any of my surroundings. The walls are covered from floor to ceiling with honey-colored wood panels. In the center of the living room hangs a light fixture decorated with deer antlers. The rustic theme continues with an animal skin rug on the floor and a stuffed deer head above the central fireplace.

I've seen this type of thing before, in old antique stores and little eateries scattered across the south, but I've never seen a dead animal used as décor in someone's home. I step closer, taking in the frightening beauty of the animal hanging on the wall. Its fur is light brown with a white underbelly, its eyes black and beady.

"Beautiful place, huh?" Nessa asks. It dawns on me I've been in the living room for several minutes now without saying anything.

"Yeah, it is." My eyes land back on the deer. "Don't you think that's a little, I don't know. Morbid?"

"Oh shit, you're not vegetarian or vegan, are you?" Harper asks.

"You've known me since we were ten," I remind her. Sometimes she forgets that she's the only one who is not a stranger to me, even if we were never close.

"Right, but *ten* was a long time ago." She dips her finger into the bubbling marinara sauce on the skillet. Licking her finger, she nods in approval, before gesturing to the deer on the wall. "The way you're looking at that thing, I wanted to make sure you're okay with eating meat."

"Yes, I eat meat," I say, not sure how the two topics connect. "It's just usually my meal doesn't stare back at me."

"There's meat in the sauce," Harper says, grabbing the skillet and turning. "That's why I asked."

"I am vegan, actually," Nessa says. She winks. "Good thing I brought stuff for salad. And I stole some of the noodles and sauce before Harper contaminated it with the murder meat."

The glass door to the left swings open, and Jackson, Colby and Matilda walk inside.

"Good," Jackson says when he sees us. "Everyone is around."

"And dinner is ready," Harper says, placing green plates in front of each empty chair. "Hope you guys are hungry."

"I'm starving," Colby says, taking a step closer to the table. He stops when he sees me, then wraps his arms around me. "Sienna, it's good to see you."

You too seems false given the circumstances. I settle on saying, "Happy to be here." Even if that isn't entirely true either.

When Colby sits at the head of the table, Matilda steps forward. She takes my hand and holds it between hers. "Jackson was right to invite you," she says. "All of us really loved Sammie. She's what brought us all together, right?"

I inhale slowly through my nose, trying to process. From behind her, I see Jackson. His arms are crossed over his chest and he's giving me a look that says, *Play nice.* I must remember why I came here and that I'm no longer alone when it comes to my mission of finding out what happened. Jackson is on my side, and he's watching the others as closely as I am.

"Coming in hot," Harper says, weaving in between the chairs with the steaming pan. She takes a spoonful of noodles and puts it on each plate. Nessa comes behind her with small salad bowls, setting them to the left of everyone's dish.

"This smells delicious, guys," Matilda says. "I hope my dessert adds up."

"I saw it in the refrigerator," Nessa says. "It looks amazing."

"Red velvet cake," she says. And before I can even finish my thought, she adds, "It was Sammie's favorite."

The sound of her name is powerful. It commands complete and immediate silence. Perhaps no one knows what to say. Perhaps they're all momentarily stunned with the reminder she isn't here. Or maybe, like me, they're lost in thought, some memory of Samantha clawing its way from the trenches, back to the forefront of our minds.

"Do you know why that was her favorite cake?" I ask the group.

Everyone stares ahead, blankly. Matilda gives a small shake of the head.

"Do tell," Jackson says, raising his glass of wine.

"On our tenth birthday, Ma and Dad ordered a cake from the local bakery. It was supposed to be a traditional white cake. Multi-colored icing. Something with butterflies or unicorns, I can't remember. Anyway, the bakery sent over the wrong cake. Dad didn't check the box until right before the party started, and by that time the bakery was closed. So, we celebrated our tenth birthday with a red velvet cake, cream cheese icing, and on the top it said: 'Happy Retirement, Al. Thanks for 30 years of service.'"

Laughs ring out from around the table. I realize the loudest is my own.

"It was this running joke for years. Who is Al and exactly who did he serve for the past three decades? Anyway, that was the first time we tried red velvet, and it's been a tradition ever since."

"So, it's your favorite cake, too?" Jackson asks.

"Yeah, I guess it is."

"That reminds me of one birthday we spent together," Colby speaks up. "I think it was her twenty-second. Maybe her twenty-third."

He goes into his story, something about a waiter and spilled margaritas. Everyone laughs, until Harper chimes in. Then Matilda, Nessa and finally Jackson. Each of them have a charming story of Samantha to tell. Some stories are familiar, others provided glimpses of my sister I never knew about, snapshots of a life too short but so sweet.

I'd be lying if I said I wasn't touched. It's obvious everyone here cared about Samantha; it's the reason Jackson gathered us all together, so we could relish her memory one more time.

At some point, in some capacity, every person here loved my sister, but at the same time, I believe they all had reason to hurt her, and at least one of them did.

Both truths can exist in the same realm.

SIXTEEN

Dishes are soaking in the sink. Wine bottles are nearly empty. Outside, darkness has fallen, heavy and complete.

"Look how bright the moon is," Nessa says, as she steps outside. We follow her, one by one, until the entire group is sitting outside, staring up at the stars.

"Wow," I say, momentarily breathless. "That's beautiful."

I've never seen a night sky like this, unobstructed by telephone wires and buildings and passing jets. It's strange to think so much peace and beauty exists only a couple of hours away from my home. Granted, my town isn't very big, but it seems totally urban when compared to a place like this. A hidden gem in the middle of nowhere.

"It feels so good to get away," Nessa says, sitting in one of the rocking chairs on the porch. "Sometimes you just need a change of scenery."

If my sister were here, I could imagine her saying the same thing.

"Samantha loved to travel," I say.

I smile, thinking of what types of activities Samantha would have tried while visiting a place like this. She loved hiking, following paths that led to beautiful destinations, thundering waterfalls and picturesque overlooks. Wherever she went, she enjoyed sampling the local cuisine, gumbo and beignets the summer our parents took us to New Orleans, tamales and Cuban food when we went to our cousin's wedding in Miami.

Our love of travel was one of the things we had in common, but, oddly enough, we rarely traveled together. Most of my trips were spontaneous, last-minute expeditions, or like my trip to Europe last summer, lengthy and too disruptive for my busy sister. I guess that's why she chose to travel with her friends. Even in college, before they all started working together, they'd sneak away for long weekends, and she'd come back sharing stories.

"Tell me about some of the places you went together," I say to her friends. "Her favorites."

"Sammie always loved the beach," Harper says. "When we were in high school, we'd always talk about moving to the ocean, learning how to surf."

"Did you two ever go surfing?"

"No." She says this with a distinct sadness. "I think the all-inclusive trips were her favorite. Pay for everything up front, then spend a week baking in the Caribbean sun."

"As long as we didn't have to sail there," Nessa says.

The five of them break out in collective laughter.

"We went on a cruise to the Bahamas to celebrate my college graduation," Matilda explains. "After that, she made it clear she'd rather fly than be stuck with seasickness on a boat."

Picturing my sister, woozy and green-faced, sailing across the Atlantic, makes me laugh, but when I lock eyes with Matilda, I quickly look away. Tonight has been pleasant, reminiscing and swapping stories, but seeing her so close to Colby still feels like a betrayal.

"Samantha would have loved this place," I say, staring up at the blinking night sky. "Had you ever traveled here before?"

"Not here," Colby says, quickly. He turns, appraising the cabin, likely comparing it to the many others they went to over the years. "We've been to this area, though. The mountains are always beautiful in the fall."

"That's why I picked this place," Jackson says. "It was the last big trip Sammie went on with the group."

"Really?"

"Yeah. It was a work retreat we hosted for some potential investors," Harper says. Like Colby, Harper looks back at the cabin, but her gaze doesn't linger. She wraps her arms around herself, although there's no breeze in sight, and breathes deeply through her nose.

"I had no idea," I say, feeling guilty that I was too busy with my own travels to keep up with hers. "When did you travel?"

"Late September, last year," Nessa says, her voice filled with sadness.

Although she doesn't say it, I assume we're all thinking the same thing: right before Samantha died. Sadness sinks in at the thought there was so much of my sister's life I missed, so much I'll never get to experience with her now. If only we'd had more time.

"The night is young," Colby says, cheerfully changing the subject. "Should we start a fire?"

He walks several feet away from the house to the round firepit, encircled in gravel beside the driveway. We follow him. Three large stumps are caddy-cornered around it. The light from the front porch just barely reaches the spot.

"Ooh, we could do s'mores," Nessa says, already walking back into the house.

"I'm already stuffed from cake," Matilda says, sitting on one of the logs. "And I don't know the first thing about starting a fire."

"Good thing we're here," Jackson says, pushing up his sleeves.

"Oh, yes. What would we do without you?" Harper says playfully, walking back in the direction of the house. "I'll bring out more wine."

I bend down and whisper in Jackson's ear, "Do you know what you're doing?"

"Not usually." He smirks. "But I'll figure it out."

With the men focusing on the firepit, it leaves me with only Matilda. I can feel her eyes on me, watching me, waiting for the precise moment to speak. She probably doesn't want to do it with the boys around, but is likely intimidated by the other women, too.

She stands. Her mouth opens, about to say something, when Jackson lets out a loud curse.

"What's wrong?" I say.

"My lighter is too weak," he says. "It's getting us nowhere."

"Just give it a second," Colby says, although I doubt he knows any more about building a fire.

"Let me go inside," I say, thankful for an opportunity to escape. "Maybe something in there can help."

"There was a gasoline can in that storage closet," Jackson says. "Down in the basement."

"Sure."

I turn quickly, before Matilda even has a chance to sit back down. I need to talk to her—I need to talk to each of them—but at the right time. I have no intention of talking to Matilda when Colby is around. After seeing the way he spoke to her earlier, when he thought they were alone, the way he grabbed her arm, I can't help wondering if he's threatening her with something, or if his mere presence would keep her from being completely honest with me.

Besides, as much as I'm reluctant to admit it, tonight has been pleasant. Hearing everyone share their stories about Samantha was a surprise. According to Jackson, it's what they planned all along. A weekend away to remember their lost friend. Even though I have ulterior motives, it was nice focusing on happier times, if only for the night.

Tomorrow, I'll get back to completing what I came here to do.

Inside the house, on my way to the basement, I pass Harper in the kitchen. She's holding out two wine bottles, trying to select one.

"Any luck with the fire outside?"

"Not really," I say. "I've been sent to get gasoline."

"That sounds dangerous." She puts one of the bottles down and turns around, searching through one of the cabinets. "Figures. Colby and Jackson always try to act macho, but I'd bet I could fix a flat before they could. Or start a fire."

"Where's Nessa?"

"Basement," she says. "She's looking for something, too."

Harper has always given off an air of confidence, even when she has no idea what she's doing. I watch her, the way she moves gracefully from one cabinet to the next, pulling out what she needs. Goblets and cocktail napkins and a corkscrew. She places them on a large wooden tray.

"I thought you hadn't been here before," I say.

"I haven't," she says, over her shoulder. "What makes you say that?"

"You know where everything is."

"It's a kitchen." Using both hands, she lifts the tray and starts making her way to the front door. "They're all the same, right?"

"Right."

Harper is likely only this domesticated on getaways like this. During the week, I assume she subsists on takeout and cleaning services. She was like that even when we were teenagers, happy to have some minions nearby to do her bidding. While the rest of us go on vacation to get away from daily responsibilities, she uses the time to practice home-making and entertaining, doing what the rest of us do every day.

"Hey, you okay?" She pauses, staring at me.

I shake my head and smile. "Just tired. It was a difficult drive."

"Well, like Colby said, the night is young. And it seems like we're all having fun." She raises the tray and walks toward the front door. "Let's enjoy it, yeah?"

I nod, watching as she goes. Harper has known me the longest. She understands just how out of my element I am, getting glimpses of their perfect lives. If it weren't for my sister, our worlds would likely never collide.

To the left, I open the door leading to the basement. I carefully descend the staircase, unable to ignore the loud groans they make with each step. It's darker here, far removed from the many windows on the main floor. Like my bedroom, the walls are wood paneled. There's a pool table in the center of the room, and along the far wall, a black leather sofa, so dark it's almost camouflaged by the shadows.

That's where I see her.

Nessa is sitting on the sofa, her head in her hands. She's sobbing.

"Are you okay?" I ask, cautiously.

She startles at the sound of my voice, standing quickly.

"Sorry," she says, wiping her face. "I thought I was alone."

"I came to get the gas can," I say, "for the fire."

Nessa refuses to look at me, her gaze instead bouncing around the room, as though searching for something. No, not searching, avoiding, as though there's a ghost here with us, some dangerous entity that remains unseen.

"I thought I heard a sound down here," she says, then laughs, nervously. "I guess it's just this old house."

Except it's not a very old house at all. It looks like a new construction to me, but I could be mistaken.

"Are you okay?" I repeat.

"Yeah. I think it was just all the stories about Sammie." She clears her throat and stands up straighter. "I miss her."

"I do, too." I reach out, my hand landing on her shoulder. She flinches.

"Sorry, I shouldn't be going over this with you." She looks away again. "It must be much harder on you."

"Samantha was a special person," I say. "Her death is hard on all of us."

She nods again, steeling herself, finding composure.

"Well, I'm going to raid the kitchen," she says. "Good thing I brought ingredients for s'mores."

"Okay."

She marches up the stairs, like she can't get away from me, or this room, fast enough. A shiver creeps up my spine. I look around the room. Maybe it's the cold air in this dank basement. Maybe it's Nessa's odd behavior. Something about this place leaves me unsettled, and I can't figure out why.

SEVENTEEN

Sometimes all you need is a strong accelerant to get a blaze going.

The fire glows red and orange, a bright orb in the middle of navy darkness. The flames make it easier to see each person's face. Nessa, biting into a s'more, laughing at something Jackson, the eternal comedian, has said. Harper sits alone on one of the logs, leaning back to pour more wine in her glass. Matilda and Colby haven't said much, but sit together, their shoulders touching innocently, but in a way that irritates me all the same.

"Anyone interested in some party favors?" Jackson asks. He reaches into his jacket and pulls out a tightly rolled joint.

"Why not?" Harper says, moving closer to him.

"This is my favorite kind of nightcap," Colby says.

I don't say anything, instead following the flattened path leading toward the side of the house, the exact spot that sits beneath my bedroom balcony. It's hard to see out here, but as I move away from the crackling firelight, my eyes adjust to the darkness. By the time I reach the trees leading into the forest, I'm able to see the hammock hanging between two tree trunks. I lower myself onto it, careful not to spill the last few sips of wine in my glass, and kick back my feet. It's hard to find balance at first, but I eventually settle into the right position, enjoy the false sense of weightlessness and the cool night air.

Lord knows, I'm no prude. I've smoked my fair share of joints, but the last thing I want to do is get high with Samantha's friends. In fact, things would work better in my favor if I was the only one to remain sober. In their inebriated state, one of them might let something slip, and I need to stay focused and clear-headed if I want to catch it.

I think of Jackson, how readily he decided to join in with the partying. Initiated it, even. He claims to be on my side, convinced one of them has something to hide, but I wonder how much of that is true. How much of what he told me in the bathroom was real? Does he really suspect one of his friends or was he only telling me what I want to hear? Most of the night, I've seen glimpses of the party boy we've all come to know. Or is that just part of his act?

Snapping twigs and crunching leaves grab my attention. The sounds are coming from somewhere close, but I can't tell if they're from the direction of the house, or from behind me, in the direction of the woods. Already, my vision has been retaken by the night. A tingle of fear climbs my spine. This place may be peaceful, but it's also isolated and remote. The kind of place where no one could hear you scream.

A dark figure appears before me. I squint, wishing I hadn't left my cell phone inside. Service might be shit, but at least I'd have some light.

"Sienna? Is that you?"

The voice belongs to Matilda.

"You caught me." The paranoia disappears, quickly replaced with annoyance. I toss back my wine glass, but there's only half a sip left. I exhale, annoyed.

"Do you have a sec?" she begins. "I wanted to talk." As I

suspected, she's been trying to confront me since after dinner. Finally, she's gotten me alone.

"Aren't you smoking with the rest of the group?"

"It's never really been my thing."

A wave of déjà vu washes over me. I've heard those words before, from Samantha's lips. I smoked my first joint when I was a freshman in high school, kept up the habit through college and beyond. I can count the times Samantha joined me on one hand. She didn't mind a drink, but smoking was never her thing. I guess Matilda feels the same way.

"What did you want to talk about?" I ask, refocusing the conversation. As much as I'm dreading talking to Matilda, with Colby distracted, this could be as good a time as any.

"I'm sure you can guess." She sits beside me on the hammock, almost toppling the entire thing over. We both reposition our weight to prevent us from falling. "I want to talk about Colby."

"There's not much to say," I say, gently placing the glass of wine on the ground. "I couldn't expect him to stay single forever."

"Neither of us imagined we'd get together the way we did." She pauses. "If anything, it was our grief over losing Sammie that brought us closer."

Sammie. Hearing her childish nickname spoken, especially by Matilda, makes my skin crawl.

I can see it all clearly in my mind. Each of her friends grieving her in their own ways, much like my parents and I mourn Samantha differently. After countless days and nights of avoiding the topic, maybe Colby and Matilda turned to one another, finding it easier to cope with their pain together. I can imagine them sharing stories about Samantha. Reminiscing on the good times. And maybe those happy memories started to morph into the present, until they were projecting those feelings onto one another, too.

Sure, I can understand it, but it still makes me queasy when I think of my sister's boyfriend and her best friend together romantically. The clichéd thing to say is that Samantha would want them to be happy, but I'm not sure that's true.

"When did it start?" I ask, pointedly.

She looks uncomfortable, as I stare at her, waiting for an answer. It took guts for her to approach me, initiate the conversation, but now I'm starting to wonder if she regrets that decision.

Matilda is confident in the way all pretty, preppy girls are. Her hair is always perfectly styled, her makeup on trend, her demeanor kind and welcoming. At the same time, Matilda is insecure, in the way all pretty, preppy girls are. She wants attention, but not for too long, and not solely for her. She doesn't trust her abilities on her own, which always separates the Matildas of the world from women like my sister. And me, for that matter. We may not always know what we're doing but we know who we are.

"When did it start?" I repeat. "You and Colby?"

"It was after Sammie died."

"When?"

"Right around the New Year. One thing led to another..." Her words trail away. She doesn't really owe me this part of the story. All I care about is that she has done right by my sister. "You have to understand how shocking her death was. It blew all our worlds apart and we were left trying to pick up the pieces."

I look away from her now, using the heels of my feet to gently swing the hammock back and forth. "I understand that part all too well."

"I'm fully aware that if Sammie were alive, there would be no relationship with Colby. And I'm okay with that. When I look at him, part of me still sees Sammie's boyfriend, too. Even if he's mine now. And an even bigger part of me wishes she was still around. I'd do anything to have her back."

The longer I listen, the more sincere she sounds. She misses her friend. There's no denying that. But as much as I want to believe the relationship with Colby didn't start until after my sister's death, I can't be sure. I know he wasn't always respectful of my sister and I'm equally mindful of what Samantha wrote about both of them in her journal.

I stand, having had enough conversations for one night. I've spoken with half of the people here and am still no closer to finding out the truth.

"I know you cared about Samantha," I say. "We all did. Thanks for coming to talk to me, Matilda."

She stands, too, and smiles.

"Please," she says. "Call me Mattie."

EIGHTEEN

SAMANTHA'S DIARY

April 2022

Some days, I consider myself incredibly lucky to work alongside my best friends.

Other days, I wish I'd moved away after graduation and started over. Like a normal person. When I meet other people at conferences, they talk about college and high school like they're the dark ages, their lives now far removed from the people they once were.

When I look around, I see the same people who've been in my circle for years. My best friend from high school. My college roommate. My sorority sister. I wonder how different my life would be if I'd decided to branch out, start over in a new place with new people, instead of reverting to what's comfortable and easy and known.

Today is one of those days where the closeness of the office environment is getting to me. Mainly, Matilda is getting to me. Or *Mattie* as everyone else calls her now.

I can still remember the first time I laid eyes on Matilda Hargrave. A spunky redhead with a beautiful face and freckled skin, impeccably dressed in brand-name clothes and matching accessories, even when the majority of our sorority sisters were wearing knock-off designers and thrift store finds.

Her eyes lit up when I revealed I'd be her Big Sister, the sorority member assigned to help ease her into her freshman year. My first year had been an eye-opener for me, but it was enjoyable because I'd quickly fallen in with a core group of friends. It wasn't long until Matilda became a part of our clique. We already spent so much time together in the sorority, it only made sense we'd forge a connection outside the sister-hood, too.

Now, Matilda looks like an entirely different person. She quickly dyed her hair, a dark black color that complemented the olive tone of her skin. Her makeup technique changes from one season to the next, following whatever is popular on social media. She still rocks designer brands, but even those have changed over time. She's now polished and professional; I only catch glimpses of the girl she used to be, naïve and eager to please.

In many ways, Matilda is the easiest friend I've ever had. When I needed someone to help manage the social media side of Sunshine Aesthetics, I couldn't think of anyone better. We don't butt heads, as Harper and I do at times, and she never dares to challenge me, as Nessa will. Yet that easy-going nature can be frustrating in a business setting. She's more than my friend. She's someone I'm entrusting with our brand. Now that we're working together nonstop, I can't help but be irritated by some of her choices, seeing her through the eyes of an employer and not just a friend.

First, there was the haircut.

After she dyed her hair in college, Matilda was known for her long, dark mane, perfectly curled and styled for every event. Then last week, she showed up to the office with a short bob. Just like mine. I almost had to do a double take; our styles look that similar. Of course, a short haircut isn't super specific, but now I'm noticing other details she's copying, too.

Like her clothes.

Again, when we first met, she already had access to nice clothes while I was stuck searching the sales rack. As a successful business owner, I pride myself on purchasing new clothes, inventing my own sense of style. Now, she's copying that, too. Matilda used to show up to the office in floral sundresses and sneakers, but lately, she's been wearing the same power suits I do. I'm talking, the exact same. The color. The brand.

After our first major success, I celebrated by purchasing a Chanel purse. I've wanted one since my high school days and was practically pinching myself over finally being able to afford one. I'd carried the purse around the office for less than a week when (guess what?) Matilda showed up with one just like it.

I know it sounds privileged and petty to complain about such things, but I guess I'd never noticed, until now, how much she aspires to be like me. That was the nature of our relationship in the beginning. She was my Little Sister; I was there to show her the way. But we're adults now, and Mattie's constant twinning is encroaching on my own identity.

Even Harper has taken notice, has started making snide remarks around the office about two Sammies. I find comments like that cringeworthy, but Matilda just laughs it off. Says something like, *Great minds, right?* It's almost like she enjoys being compared to me. When we were in college, fine. But as adults? It just feels weird.

Matilda and I don't just have similar tastes. It is becoming increasingly obvious that she's trying to copy my every move. Even the videos she posts online to recruit clients look more and more like the videos I created when we started the company. On one level, I suppose that's what I'm paying her to do, expand the company brand. Lately, she's been going beyond her normal responsibilities as the social media manager. She's been pitching ideas in our business meetings, talking about strategies that have nothing to do with her area of expertise.

Sometimes, I'll even walk by her office and see her working on vision boards, directions we could take the company in two, five, ten years. If Nessa were doing that sort of thing, I'd pay no mind, but Matilda should know better. It makes me wonder if the plans aren't for me or Sunshine Aesthetics at all. My biggest fear is that one day she'll stop copying my fashion sense, and start coming after the business I created, poaching our clients.

They say imitation is the greatest form of flattery, but I'm starting to wonder if there's something more sinister at play... if Matilda is trying to move me out of the way, so she can take my place.

NINETEEN

SIENNA

After our talk, Mattie said she was turning in for the night. Once alone, I contemplate everything she said to me, comparing it to what was written in the journal.

Even though Matilda insists she didn't start dating Colby until recently, instinct tells me not to believe her. Samantha's gut was wrong: Matilda wasn't after her business, but potentially, her man. She was, however, right about the eerie similarities between them, their style and behavior. But in my eyes, Mattie will always be a cheaper, knock off version of my sister.

The rest of the group has splintered off, going in different directions. Nessa and Harper are in the basement, playing billiards. Jackson and Colby remain on the front porch drinking and smoking.

Unlike the rest, I crave privacy, moments alone. It was another fundamental difference between Samantha and me. The eternal extrovert, she longed to be around other people, found strength in those around her. I was the opposite, needing moments of quiet and calm to center myself. It's not that I'm incapable of having relationships with others—the bond with my sister proves that—but I require solitude, time for reflection.

That's a positive detail of a place like this; surrounded by woods and mountains, there are moments when it feels as though I'm the only person on earth. The feeling isn't as lonely as you might expect.

I replay the conversation with Matilda like an engineer might survey a structure, searching for weak points, contemplating its reliability. Learning about the new relationship was shocking; it's easy to point my suspicions at Mattie and Colby, but I have to remember that alarms were raised before I arrived here, long before I knew they were a couple. Before I even found my sister's diary, if I'm being honest.

If their relationship started before Samantha's death, it provides them both with motive to want her out of the way, but the rest of the group has motives, too. I can't let my outrage at Colby and Mattie's relationship cloud my vision.

"Taking in the view?" Jackson exits the house through the sliding glass doors, joining me by the wooden railing.

"I've seen better," I say.

"That doesn't surprise me," he says. "You have more stamps on your passport than I have notches on my bedpost."

"And you think that's something to brag about?"

He shrugs, playfully. He props himself up on the wooden railing and lights a cigarette.

"Get down," I warn him. "You've been drinking and it's dark."

"I'm fine."

And yet I can't stop thinking about how easily Samantha lost her own life in a fall. Surely, she wasn't careless enough to lean against the railing. Then again, according to the medical examiner, my sister was half-drunk, like Jackson.

"It's dangerous," I say.

Whether it's the tone of my voice or the look on my face, I'm not sure, but Jackson seems to follow my train of thought, to remember why we're all here, how my sister's fall, accidental or not, ended in tragedy. He hops off the railing.

"I wanted to check in on you before calling it a night." He inhales deeply and releases a thick plume of smoke. "I guess I feel responsible in some ways, seeing as I invited you here."

"I'm a grown woman, Jackson. I can fend for myself."

"I'd say you could fend for both of us." He smirks and takes a sip of his beer. "Did you get a chance to talk to anyone tonight?"

"A little. Nessa and I talked about business. Then Matilda ambushed me while the rest of you were getting high."

"And?"

"Neither one of them came out and admitted any wrongdoing, but, of course, I never expected things to be that simple. They both talked about how they missed Samantha. Blah, blah, blah."

"You don't believe them?"

"I don't know what to believe. The only thing I have that tells me whether someone is lying is Samantha's diary, and she didn't do me the pleasure of naming her killer in the journal."

"*If* there is a killer."

"Right. If." I look ahead, out into the dark bramble of treetops. "I know it sounds like I'm losing my mind. Like I can't accept Samantha's death, so I'm making things up, but I know my sister better than everyone. There's a reason she left me that voice mail. And a reason she left her diary for me to find. Whether it's rational or not, everything inside me is telling me I'll find my answers here."

Jackson flicks his cigarette off the back deck and takes a step closer, placing a warm hand on my shoulder. "I don't think you're losing your mind. Something about Sammie's death bothers me, too."

I turn to face him, turning my back on the forest. "Do you

think we loved her the most? Maybe that's why we can't let any of this go."

"I'd say we definitely loved her the most." That charming smile spreads across his face. "But that doesn't mean we're being irrational. The rest of the group is hiding something. You know that because of the diary."

I look away, thinking. "Right. They all had secrets, but don't all of us? Maybe it's wrong to be using their secrets against them. They're just words. Samantha's thoughts and feelings in the moment. Even she didn't come out and say she thought someone was trying to kill her."

She only hinted that something was wrong.

I need you. Now.

"Everything happened so fast towards the end," he says. "She was here one day, and then gone the next."

"But what was happening? I don't know. Her entries were few and far between after the summer, and then the final pages were ripped out, like even she didn't have time to write about what was going on."

"I don't know."

"But you should. You were here, around Samantha every day. And the rest of the group."

Jackson looks down, his thick hair falling in front of his face. "I wasn't around as much as I should have been. That's something I'll always regret."

"Tell me about it." I cross my arms, looking back out at the darkened view. "I was getting wasted halfway across the world while my sister was back here. Dealing with everything on her own."

"Don't blame yourself." Jackson touches my shoulder again. "Sammie wanted you to go out and have adventures."

"No, she didn't," I admit. "I should have been here with her."

"You are a great sister. Even now, you won't give up on her."

"But it doesn't matter. Even if I'm right, and one of her friends is responsible for her death, it won't bring her back."

Jackson turns me around to face him. "Sammie loved you, Sienna. So much. And I loved her. We can get to the bottom of this together."

I stare into his eyes, searching, for what, I don't know. Maybe I need the confidence in myself to keep going, to not give up on my suspicions, no matter how irrational they may seem.

"You don't realize how happy I am that you decided to come," Jackson says. He smiles, and for the first time during our conversation, I'm reminded of how inebriated he is. I get a strong whiff of booze and weed that makes me want to pull away, but Jackson won't let go. He holds my shoulders tighter. "You look so much like her."

Jackson leans down, pulling me closer, until his lips are on mine. Soft and timid at first, the kiss morphs into something more passionate.

I push him away, wiping at my mouth with the back of my hand.

"What the hell are you doing?"

"I... I don't know." He stumbles over his words. "I just thought—"

"Are you telling me what I want to hear so you can sleep with me?"

"No. That's not it. I'm..."

His words crumble into murmurs. I realize I'm putting my trust in a partier, a playboy, a drunk. This entire conversation— maybe every conversation we've had today—means nothing.

I rush back toward the house, stopping suddenly when I see Nessa standing behind the glass door. How long has she been there? Did she hear everything? See everything?

I pull back the door and march inside, bumping her shoulder as I pass.

"Sienna, are you okay?" she calls after me, but I ignore her.

I hurry down the hallway and into my bedroom, locking the door behind me. I sit on the bed and begin to sob.

Tonight has made one thing abundantly clear: I can't trust anyone here.

TWENTY

TROY

Troy makes his traditional breakfast of eggs, toast and bacon, making extra meat for Twister and Jennings out back. He showers and gets dressed.

Outside, he considers having a second cup of coffee so he can enjoy the early morning sunrise but thinks better of it. High winds have picked up during the night, blowing over most of the light furniture and wood on his front porch. After cleaning up the mess, he decides to ride into town, get his responsibilities over with for the day.

Today he is going to visit the only family he has left. His father. Really, the only family he's ever had. No brothers and sisters. No cousins, aunts or uncles. His mother had taken off when he was only a toddler, and his memories of her are hazy at best. Sometimes, Troy doesn't know if he is remembering glimpses of his mother or getting those images confused with clips of other women he's seen on television.

It never bothered him, having only one parent. His father provided more than enough love and guidance for two people. Despite all Troy had grown up without, he never felt like he was at a disadvantage. It is part of the reason he remains loyal, never skipping a Saturday visit.

Troy goes by the local grocery store to pick up some necessities. While there, he stops by the in-house florist and purchases a bouquet of flowers. Daisies and an assortment of smaller flowers that look like they are on the verge of dying.

"How's the family?" the woman working the checkout line asks. Mrs. Rutters. Troy is so busy putting his purchases on the conveyor belt, he doesn't recognize her at first.

"All good," Troy says with a smile.

Mrs. Rutters has memory problems and often forgets about what happened. When she gets confused, it's easier to go along with what she says than it is to correct her. Easier for her, and easier for Troy.

He gives a wave and pushes open the glass doors before she can say anything else.

Point A is never far away from Point B in a place like this. Ten minutes later, Troy is pulling his truck up a hill. He gets out of his car and lowers the chain pulled across the entrance so that he can keep driving.

He makes it to a clearing, only a few slate-colored stones visible in the tall, yellowed grass. Slowly, he makes his way across the field, placing the flowers beside a medium-sized headstone. The grave reads: *Troy Adams Sr. 1958-2018*

"Happy Saturday, Dad," Troy says.

He sits in silence for a long, long while.

TWENTY-ONE

SIENNA

It feels like something sharp is poking at my eyelids, but it's only the intrusive rays of sunlight cutting through the glass door, disrupting my peaceful slumber.

Surprisingly, last night was the best sleep I've had in a while. In the past year, there have been countless nights of tossing and turning, even bouts of insomnia, where my brain was so wired, I wasn't able to turn it off.

Perhaps it was the heavy down comforter, the cool temperature or the serene quiet outside my balcony, but something made it easier for me to sleep. Maybe my body is simply preparing itself, ensuring a full rest before I take on my goal for the weekend.

As the faces of my other house guests flash before my mind, I remember last night, the awkward kiss Jackson and I shared on the porch. He'd had a lot to drink—I'm starting to think that's an excuse he often leans on—but nothing else warranted that behavior. It makes me question his real motives, whether he's really here to help me uncover the truth, or if he has other ideas.

Someone knocks against my bedroom door.

"Just a second," I shout, pulling the covers up to my chest and swiping at my hair. "Come in."

Jackson walks into the room, a steaming mug in each hand. I sit up straighter. After what happened, Jackson is the last person I want to see me in this state. Underdressed and vulnerable. When's the last time I've shared a bed with a man, even if it is just a morning coffee? A year or more? Back when I was traveling.

"Are you a coffee drinker?" he asks.

I clear my throat. "Not usually, but I'll take one this morning."

I take the cup, the ceramic warm in my palms. An awkward silence covers the room. Neither of us look at each other, despite being the only ones here. The morning cry of a bird on the other side of the sliding glass door is the only sound.

"I want to apologize," he says, "for last night."

"I didn't know you were interested in me that way. I wouldn't have come if I—"

"I'm not interested in you," he cuts me off. He lowers his head, running a hand through his mop of hair. "I'd had too much to drink. It was a mistake."

"You can't blame it on the alcohol."

"But it's true. Alcohol has been my problem for years. It brings out this other side of me, a person I don't want to be."

I take a sip of my coffee, thinking. Jackson has always been charming, far more likable than the rest of my sister's friends, but there is another side of him. Before he kissed me, I believed he actually valued what I had to say, what I came here to do, but now I'm not so sure.

"I've been trying to get a handle on it," he says, his gaze still fixed on the floor. "I even went to rehab once."

"I had no idea," I say. "When?"

"Before Sammie died. The program seemed to work, for a while, but after she died, I didn't care about anything."

Samantha never mentioned anything about Jackson going to rehab in her journal. It proves that even though she revealed some of her friends' secrets, there are still other things I don't know about them. Motives could exist I know nothing about.

I place my coffee on the bedside table, pulling my legs closer to my body.

"When Samantha died, my first reaction was that something didn't make sense. I couldn't understand how she'd fallen, how she'd had so much alcohol in her system when she barely drank. And then there was that voice mail. She sounded so distraught. I was convinced there was another reason for her death, but no one believed me. They said no one was with her when she died and there weren't any reasons someone would want to hurt her. My parents, the police. They all made it seem like I was latching onto irrational ideas because of my grief.

"And then I found her journal, and I realized there was a lot about the people in her life we didn't know. Things that worry me. Things that worried Samantha. For the first time, it felt like I had proof someone might have wanted to hurt her. When I came to you with my suspicions, you were the first person who didn't tell me I was crazy for thinking this way. I thought I finally had someone on my side."

"I am on your side, Sienna," he says. "I promise."

"Last night, when you kissed me, it felt like you were only telling me what I want to hear," I say.

"I crossed a boundary last night; one I won't cross again." He looks at me now, directly into my eyes. "I believe you that the rest of the group is hiding something. One of them, all of them, might have been involved in Samantha's death. I'm willing to help you. Whatever you need."

I place my hand over his and squeeze. "Thank you."

Even though last night was unsettling, Jackson made it a point to apologize. Even if he hadn't, the fact someone else believes I might be right, that I'm not crazy, is enough for me to forgive him.

He takes another sip of his coffee, gazing out the sliding glass door. "Do you have a game plan?"

"I'm still taking my time talking to everyone. I haven't spoken to any of them in more than a year. Some even longer. I'm hoping they'll keep talking long enough to put a foot in their mouths and then I can confront them with the journal."

"I'll have your back when you do."

He places his palm over my knee and squeezes. Once again, I'm happy to have him as an ally.

As he opens the front door, he pauses and looks back at me.

"You said the last few pages of the journal were torn out."

I nod.

He looks down. "That doesn't sit well with me. Something must have been so bad Sammie didn't want anyone else to know."

"That. Or someone else took the pages."

"Either way, it isn't good."

That brings up another point—who would have, or could have, taken the missing pages? Samantha must have been the person who hid the diary; she's the only person who knew about our hiding spot in the broken window seat. If she was hiding the journal, why rip out the last few pages? Was there something written in the diary she didn't want me to know, or is it just some useless coincidence? The questions linger, the answers just beyond my grasp, like all the other puzzles surrounding my sister's death.

Jackson remains at the door another moment before he exits the room. There isn't much left to be said to each other. We both have our suspicions, but we won't get any answers until we investigate.

I fall back on my pillow. To the left, my eyes land on the framed picture I brought of Samantha and me.

"What was *your* secret?" I whisper, staring at my sister's smiling face.

I keep looking and waiting, even though I know there will be no response.

TWENTY-TWO

There's nothing more appealing than the smell of frying bacon. And I know from working at Roth Family Cleaners, no stain is harder to eliminate.

After I shower and get dressed, I round the corner, following the inviting scent, my stomach starting to rumble. I freeze when I catch Colby and Matilda in the kitchen, staring into each other's eyes like two lovesick teenagers.

Colby sees me first out of the corner of his eye. He immediately stiffens and clears his throat.

"Morning, Sienna!" Matilda says when she notices me. Her voice is too cheery and welcoming, especially this early in the morning. We might have had a one-on-one conversation last night, but I still don't consider her a friend. I know I can't trust her.

"Where is everyone?"

"Still haven't seen Nessa. Jackson and Harper went out." She turns around facing the stove. "We're making breakfast for everyone. Eggs. Bacon. Biscuits."

"That's... unnecessary."

"It was part of the plan," Colby says. "Each of us volunteered to make a meal. Nessa and Harper went last night—"

"And now it's our turn," Matilda cuts him off.

She's trying to sound light and airy, but there's something untrusting and patronizing about Colby's tone, as though the sole reason he brought up their little cooking schedule is to remind me I wasn't an original guest. I don't belong.

"Are you hungry now?" Matilda asks, desperate to keep me in the conversation.

"I'm going outside for a bit. Enjoy the morning air."

"Have fun," Colby barks over his shoulder, sounding genuinely happy because I'm leaving. I see Matilda hit him with an elbow as I exit.

"Jackass," I whisper under my breath.

Colby and I never really got along. We tolerated one another more than anything, for Samantha's sake. I thought she was too good for him, but truthfully, I think I would have thought that about any guy she decided to date.

As brilliant as Samantha was in most areas of her life, her taste in men was always lacking. From afar, the guys she dated seemed ideal. Handsome, smart, wealthy. But they all seemed to have demons that, at least in my mind, erased their attractive traits.

My sister spent most of high school pining after a boy named Cameron. He might have been the most popular athlete in school, but even then I knew my sister could do better. There were some other boys here and there, mostly minor flings. She met Colby her freshman year of college, and the two were together ever since. My parents were hopeful they'd soon get married, an idea that made me want to vomit.

Having Colby here, after her death, with a new girl... just the sight of him makes my insides squirm with anger.

"Watch out!"

I look up just in time for an enlarged badminton birdie to fly past my nose. It lands on the ground beside my foot.

"Sorry about that," Jackson says, chasing the birdie.

"Almost clipped you," Harper says.

"What on earth are you two doing?"

"There's a game closet off the back deck. We found these inside," Harper says. "Aren't they massive?"

In fact, both rackets and the birdie are at least five times the original size, big enough that two people could hit back and forth without needing a net.

"Usually, I don't break a sweat this early in the morning," Jackson says. He leans forward, putting a hand on his hip as though he's at least three decades older than he is. "You're killing me, Harper."

"Come on. Don't be such a baby."

"Seriously. I'm done for the day. Maybe after I have a few drinks in me I won't be as bothered. I'm going to wash up and eat some breakfast."

"Matilda and Colby will be thrilled," I say, voice full of snark. "They're cooking breakfast for everyone, you know."

Jackson gives me a look before he hobbles back inside. I turn to find Harper still standing there holding her giant racket. I hadn't intended to make a comment about the couple in front of her, but I wasn't thinking.

"Still struggling with the lovebirds, I see."

"Can you blame me?"

"No. She's your sister. We understand your anger. All of us had the same reaction as you at first."

Maybe they did, but they didn't voice it. If I've learned anything from hanging out with my sister's friends, it's that their true feelings and their overt reactions are two totally different things.

"You've known Samantha longer than all the others," I say.

"How did you react when you found out he'd moved on so soon?"

"It made sense to me. I mean, Mattie has been structuring her life after Samantha's for years."

"What do you mean?"

"Come on, it's obvious. *Sammie and Mattie.* The way they style their hair. Now she even has her boyfriend. Matilda was trying to replace Sammie years before she died."

Samantha said as much in her diary, complaining that Matilda was trying to hijack her style, her ideas, her life. Still, Harper's word choice bothers me: *replace Samantha.* Was Matilda's friendship with my sister really that superficial? Did she care about Samantha at all, or did she only care about being like her?

"Maybe she isn't trying to be like Samantha," I say, trying to move the conversation along, back to Harper herself. "I mean, when two people spend time together, they're liable to rub off on one another, wouldn't you say?"

Harper and my sister became friends when they were in middle school. They'd both been selected for the Junior Varsity cheer team; I hadn't made the cut. Granted, I didn't want to be a cheerleader. I'd only tried out because Ma insisted. Back then, our parents believed because we shared the same birthday, we were meant to go through every stage of life together, enjoy all the same activities, until it became clear to everyone, especially me, that Samantha and I were destined for different things.

Anyway, because this was the first thing Samantha did without me by her side, Harper became her best friend. Cheer practice led to weekend visits led to sleepovers. In all the areas of Samantha's life I resented, Harper was more than happy to take my place. Most people would assume that resulted in jealousy. If anything, I was relieved Samantha had someone else by her side. It meant I didn't have to do it.

And even though my sister had found a new best friend, one who stayed with her until the end of her life, it never weakened the relationship we had with one another. I think that is the part of our siblinghood people struggle to understand. That Samantha and I were so different and yet our bond was unbreakable.

Samantha's new friendship did result in some changes. Harper is what most people would call a prep or a princess. Looking back, she was a mean girl. And some of that mean spiritedness rubbed off on my kind, bright sister. Not enough that people would remember. If you were to ask most of the people she'd gone to school with, I think they'd remember her as funny, shy. It was her bitch of a best friend you had to worry about...

You'd have had to really know Samantha to see the changes in her. The way she'd get roped into bullying other girls at school; I don't think she ever said anything herself, but she certainly didn't speak against Harper or their other friends. Or in high school, when the cheer squad was busted for smuggling alcohol on the road trip to nationals. Harper might have been the one to bring the booze, but Samantha and the others got in trouble for it.

Some of those antics earned Samantha, Harper and their friends a certain reputation, but my sister was never a bad girl. She was a *young* girl, trying on different personas until she found the one that fit. That's the way I saw it, anyway. The bad behavior toned down by the time they were in college. Or so I thought. Staring at Harper now, I wonder what other secrets she has up her sleeve.

"I talked to Matilda last night," I say. "She told me things didn't start up with Colby until after Samantha had died. Months after, actually. That they leaned on each other during their grief."

Harper makes a face and turns around.

"What is it?" I ask.

She sighs. "Those two were hooking up long before your sister died."

Harper thinks she knows things. Usually, it's only something she's pretending to have known after some big revelation comes to light. She won't pass the opportunity to stir the pot.

"How do you know?"

She crosses her arms, the badminton racket hanging from one hand. "Because I caught them."

TWENTY-THREE

SAMANTHA'S DIARY

July 2022

Can someone remind me why Harper Toll has been my best friend for the past decade?

I love her, of course. After all this time, she's like family. In fact, whenever we get into arguments, it's like two sisters fighting. Hell, I fight with her more than I do with my own sister. Sometimes history with someone just provides more reasons to not like them, and I'm afraid that's becoming the case with us.

In typical Harper fashion, the whole thing started over one of her ideas.

Back in January, when we were working on our mission statements and vision boards for the new year, she suggested we hold quarterly reviews with each employee. I thought it was a great idea. A way for us to hold people accountable and avoid resentment building all at once.

But also in typical Harper fashion, she likes to throw out rules that apply to everyone but her. Just like when we were in high school, and she'd provide detailed feedback for each member of the squad, but never be open to what others were saying about her. She can't handle criticism. It's like she expected us to improve everyone at the company besides her.

"How would you adjust your performance?" I asked her, sitting in the conference room between our two offices. It was an open-ended question, one that shouldn't have led to an argument. It was the same question I asked every other member of our team this week.

"My performance?"

"We're doing the quarterly check-ins," I reminded her. "Like you suggested."

"Do you think there's something wrong with my performance?"

"No."

And again, I tried explaining we were doing this with everyone. For whatever reason, Harper felt she should be exempt. Losing her sense of entitlement would be one major improvement, but with Harper, I think it just comes with the territory.

Truthfully, even I had started to question what Harper brought to the company. Each of our employees has their own strengths, their own way of impacting the business as a whole. Mattie shines on social media, Jackson and Colby woo the investors we need, and the whole thing would fall apart without Nessa's coding skills. What does Harper provide? A joke from time to time, a smiling face every day when we're gossiping between meetings. Right now, she's providing little more than a massive headache.

Back to the fight, she said, sounding like a whiny teenager, "If you think I'm not doing my job, you can just say it."

I mean, really? Would she have reacted that way to any other boss? Or was it just me? Maybe that history between us, being there for each other's first kisses and first periods, meant she'd never have the same respect for me she'd have for any other employer.

"Your role has been questioned by others working in the company."

"Who?"

I refused to tell her. Firstly, because it doesn't matter. When it comes to my employees, all final decisions come to Nessa and me. Secondly, because the teenage girl in me still enjoys the entertainment of watching Harper squirm when she doesn't get her way.

"It's that little wannabe, isn't it?" she said. "Mattie. She wants me out so she can have more control."

"I didn't say that—"

"Then tell me, who is criticizing me?"

I closed my eyes tightly. This is the hard part about sitting in the boss's chair. There comes a time when difficult tasks are no one's responsibility other than my own.

"I'm questioning how you're helping the business, honestly. You work closely with Mattie and Nessa and Colby. But what is it you do?"

"Whatever needs to be done."

"Right." I looked down. Gosh, this was so hard, saying this to my oldest friend. "I think it would be good if you took more initiative. Maybe started a client list of your own, people you could directly help... instead of only working behind the scenes."

"This isn't you talking," she said, plainly. "You've never once questioned my work ethic."

Perhaps I should have, a long time ago. All my time with Harper has taught me one thing: if she can't be the top dog, the queen bee, the boss, she fades into the back. I was trying to help her, improve her potential, although she clearly didn't take it that way.

"Someone else is putting these ideas in your head," she continues. "Just tell me who."

"That isn't productive, Harper. Pointing fingers at other people won't help the environment around the office."

"Maybe I'm not the person here you should be worried about."

Her comment, as broad and aloof as it was, stopped me cold.

"What does that mean?"

Was she referencing Jackson and his substance abuse? I always worried about his partying getting out of hand, but it wasn't to the point it would tarnish the business, was it? Or was she talking about something else? A liability or betrayal I didn't know about?

"Don't worry about it," Harper said, slowly raising herself from the conference table. "I just think it's important to remember who's in your corner, otherwise it might come back to bite you."

"Is that a threat?"

"Of course, it isn't," she said. "Just a little advice between friends."

The conversation never found a resolution. Instead of going through the motions of conversation, like every other employee did, Harper had to make it more dramatic. Instead of advocating for her own performance, she was on a mission to find out who was criticizing her, even though I kept insisting she had nothing to worry about. Some of our other friends are threatened by the fact Harper and I have such a lengthy history, that's all.

Still, it might be that long history at the root of her outburst. We're both blessed and cursed with knowing who the other was before we were successful adults. Back in high school, Harper was a shining star. Cheer captain. Volleyball captain. Prom queen. And I was her best friend, constantly by her side. If you'd asked us then who would have ended up working for whom, Harper would have been pegged as the boss, hands down.

Something changed in college. Whatever spark Harper had as a teenager fizzled out. Sure, she was still beautiful and smart and funny, but so were dozens of other girls. She no longer stood out against the crowd, and she no longer stood out beside me. She didn't even make it into the same sorority as me, a fact I try to never bring up; it was the first time Harper had ever experienced rejection in her life, and it's probably the real reason she doesn't like Mattie.

I'm a far cry from the young girl I was when I first befriended Harper, and I've worked hard to get where I am. I've landed the boyfriend, the scholarships, the business opportunities. And even though Harper always claims to support me, sometimes I wonder how hard it must be for her to constantly be in the shadows, watching me succeed.

If situations were reversed, I'd be there for her. I *was* there for her.

Yet, here we are, building a business together, and I don't feel like the feelings are reciprocated.

TWENTY-FOUR

SIENNA

A burning sensation climbs up my neck, warming my ears and cheeks.

"What do you mean you caught them?"

Harper drops the racket and takes a step back, sitting on the rod-iron chair beside the house. I remain standing, anger and adrenaline rushing through me.

"It was the Fourth of July. The group went to this new venue by the lake for fireworks and dinner and drinks. She might have told you about it."

I remember, vaguely. As much as I'd like to remember all the details of the conversations we had together before my trip overseas, I tuned out a lot of what she said. I was busy thinking about my own adventures.

I shake my head, refocusing on whatever story Harper is going to tell. "Go on."

"By the time the fireworks had ended, everyone was plastered. Understandably. I mean, we were celebrating the company, the holiday. Everything. Samantha was happy that night. We wanted to get a picture of the six of us, but it probably would have been a better idea to have done it earlier in the night. Samantha was with Jackson and Nessa at the bar. I was going around looking for Colby and Mattie.

"I stepped outside, figuring Colby had gone out back for a smoke. He tries to be like Jackson whenever he drinks, you know. That's where I saw them. They were leaned up against the wall of the building, making out."

"What did you say to them?"

"They never saw me," she says. "I went back inside before they saw."

"You should have confronted them."

"And cause a big scene?" Harper shakes her head. "I was wasted. We all were. I figured maybe I was confused."

"But you're sober now. You were sober the next morning. You know what you saw, right?"

Harper waits for a beat. "Yes, it was definitely them."

"What did Samantha say when you told her?"

Another pause. "I never told her."

"*What?*" A new wave of anger washes over me. "She's your best friend."

"We're all friends! I didn't know what to do."

"But you and Samantha have known each other the longest. Matilda was brought into the group because of Samantha. You should have had her back."

She looks down. "Given our history, I wasn't sure I was the best person to tell her Colby might be cheating."

I'd almost forgotten the origin story for why I disliked Harper so much. Sure, there was the catty, mean girl crap most girls my age went through, but there was a concrete experience I believed spoke to Harper's character too.

It was our senior year of high school. Samantha had spent most of the spring semester flirting with a guy on the soccer team. Cameron Jones. Everyone thought he was one of the dreamiest guys at school. Samantha had crushed on him for years, and by the time they were both seniors, it became clear he felt the same way.

Their courtship was innocent and slow-moving. Samantha had had boyfriends before, but no one she was really serious about. Until Cameron. It appeared they were on the road to making their relationship official. They went to the Spring Homecoming Dance together—as friends—but she was giddy as could be when their night ended with a kiss. They were even talking about attending prom together at the end of the year.

And then Harper interfered. Harper, her best friend, who had never even taken a second glance at Cameron, suddenly decided she had feelings for him. She told Samantha as much. Thing is, Cameron wasn't her boyfriend. She didn't have grounds to tell him what he should or shouldn't do, but the bigger betrayal, in my opinion, came from Harper. She knew exactly how my sister felt, and she went after her crush anyway.

After a soccer team victory, Harper accompanied Cameron to an afterparty and they ended up sleeping together. Samantha was devastated.

"You deserve better," I remember telling her. Samantha was in my room, sitting on my bed with the black sheets and *The Nightmare Before Christmas* comforter, crying uncontrollably. "From both of them."

"Harper likes him, too," she said. "She can't control how she feels."

"Yes, she can." I was adamant. "She knew how you felt about him. We all did."

"It's not like he's my boyfriend. He chose her over me, and it hurts."

"If she were a real friend, she never would have made him choose," I said, thinking this might finally be the situation that freed Harper's claws from my sister's back. She'd influenced her behavior for years, but this? It was the ultimate betrayal.

"Harper and I are going to Westwood in the fall. Things

probably wouldn't have even lasted with Cameron. I can't throw away years of friendship over some dumb guy."

That's exactly what Harper did, I thought to myself, but I stayed quiet. I wasn't going to make Samantha choose between me and her best friend. Mainly, because at that moment she needed comfort. Secondly, because I wasn't sure who she might pick.

The incident was so long ago—almost ten years now—I hardly thought of it anymore, until I was reading through Samantha's journal. Even now, the incident feels small when stacked against my other suspicions, but it is the reason I stopped trusting Harper.

"What happened with Cameron was a long time ago," I say to Harper. "We're adults. If you came to her, she would have believed you."

"I wanted to tell her, okay? I really did. But there was never a good moment. After the summer, we worked fourteen- and fifteen-hour days. All of us. Telling her about what I'd seen would have only added to the stress we were all feeling."

"But she was your friend, Harper. Surely whatever she was going through was more important than the business."

"I kept an eye on them. Mattie and Colby, I mean. I paid close attention whenever we were in meetings, whenever we went out together. I never saw anything else suspicious, so I wrote it off as a drunken mistake. I didn't think they were having an affair under Samantha's nose."

I'm frustrated by all of it. If the roles were reversed, nothing would have stopped Samantha from letting her friend know the truth, but just as she wrote in her journal, her loyalty wasn't reciprocated. I think of all the sacrifices Samantha made over the years, her generosity in inviting her friends to join her business, and how none of them gave her the respect she deserved in return.

Just yesterday, Matilda swore to me she hadn't started her

relationship with Colby until after Samantha's death. I'm angry at Colby for betraying my sister. And I'm angry that Harper, my sister's oldest friend, wouldn't tell her the truth.

"Well, clearly, they kept things up. They were sleeping with each other right under everyone's noses."

"That's why I wasn't surprised when they started dating," she says. "I was angry, but not surprised."

Harper doesn't know what angry is. By the looks of it, she doesn't understand loyalty either. I think of all the times she stirred the pot, fed off other people's drama, but when she was confronted with information that would matter to someone she cares about, she chose to look the other way.

I turn on my heels, marching back toward the house.

"Where are you going?" Harper asks.

"I'm doing what you should have done over a year ago," I say. "I'm confronting Colby."

TWENTY-FIVE

SAMANTHA'S DIARY

August 2022

It's official. My life has become a cliché.

Overworked, overtired businesswoman trying to make a name for herself in a male-dominated industry with a (drumroll, please) cheating boyfriend.

Okay, okay, I don't know for a fact Colby is cheating, but I can't shake this feeling that something is off. We've been together for eight years now. We could just be hitting a slow spot. It happens, right? Or maybe it's the fact we're working together. Our interactions in the office are so important, it's easy to overlook the romantic side of our relationship. Both those explanations are completely rational. And yet, this feeling... it won't go away. Something gnawing its way through me from the inside out.

I figured I'd write down my suspicions here. Maybe seeing all the clues in one spot will let me know if I'm crazy. Or not.

First and foremost, there's the sex. Or lack thereof. Another cliché, right? Career-minded woman can't meet her man's sexual needs, so he looks elsewhere.

It's not like our sex life has ever been anything amazing (dear God, don't let him see this), but we at least had a routine. Sex was comfortable, expected.

We've slept together twice since July. Even in the driest of dry spells that's weird.

And I'm not the one saying no. He comes in every night talking about how tired he is. Or that he has a headache. His new medication is making him woozy.

On our anniversary, I squeezed myself into one of those ridiculous red lacy getups, thinking the change in routine might get us out of our funk. He took one look at me and started apologizing profusely, talking about how he'd thrown up at the office and didn't want to ruin our night.

Well, Colby, the night was ruined! Not only did I not get laid, but I had to squeeze out of the lingerie and settle for my comfy plaid pajamas. Not exactly the romantic evening I had planned.

His behavior has been off, too.

He keeps going on and on about this potential investor, Roy Balding. He's had meeting after meeting with the guy trying to secure his investment. With a bigger advertising budget, we could target more high-profile clients and even hire more staff to do our jobs for us.

The thing is, I enjoy working! It's why I started my own company. I thought inviting Colby and the others to join me was a good idea, but the past year has shown maybe that's wrong.

Anyway, back to Colby. He's obsessed with this Roy Balding guy because he was once featured in a listicle in *Forbes*. He's gone to countless meetings and Balding's beautiful, busty assistant is always in attendance. I know because she posts their meetings on social media, which is basically the same as getting cheated on in my own home. Insta and TikTok are my realm! It's like she's flashing it in my face.

Maybe I'm being paranoid. He might not be sleeping with Balding's assistant. Or anyone. But this isn't the Colby I used to know. Sometimes I think if it weren't for our business ties and the condo we share and our tight-knit circle of friends he'd leave me.

Our friends. I worry about them, too. It's awful to say, but sometimes I question Harper's loyalty. It's been ages since she betrayed me with Cameron, but once you've been burned, the scar never really fades. Of course, we were kids then. She wouldn't dream of interfering with a real relationship.

But am I even in a real relationship anymore? It feels like I have a glorified roommate I can't stand half the time. Hell, it's like having a husband!

Maybe my paranoia stems from something else. My mind often revisits that New Year's conversation with Jackson. I was quick to shoot him down, but sometimes I wonder if that was a mistake. I know, it's awful to make these accusations about Colby when I'm still having thoughts about Jackson—but I'd never act on them. Perhaps it's just natural. If two people can grow apart, it only makes sense that two others can grow closer, right?

I don't know. Maybe the stress of work is making me lose my mind. Another cliché that only ever seems to hound professional women, never the men.

Here's what I do know. If my intuition is right, and Colby is banging the secretary or anyone else, I won't stand for it. That is where the clichés will stop.

I might be able to handle his mediocre lovemaking and his mood swings and his insecurities. That's what you do for someone you love. But I know my worth. If Colby is unfaithful, he'll lose me, our home and his stocks in the company.

That's a promise.

TWENTY-SIX

SIENNA

When I storm inside the house, Jackson, Nessa and Matilda are seated at the table. Colby remains in the kitchen, a frying pan in hand. They all turn at the sound of my arrival, like a strong wind gives way to a storm to come.

"Colby, we need to talk." I don't sound like myself. My voice is coarse with anger. "Now."

Around the table, everyone shares confused looks with raised eyebrows. The tension that's been building since our arrival has finally erupted. Colby walks to the sink and drops the pan. He turns on the faucet, the water hissing when it hits the hot metal.

"Everything okay?" he asks, nonchalantly.

My look should say enough so I don't answer. I continue staring, piercing him with hateful eyes, tapping my foot impatiently.

He wipes his hand with a dishrag on the counter before walking in my direction. He stops in front of me, raising his hands as though to say, *Lead the way*.

I walk forward, exiting through the front door so we can sit on the porch. It's brighter out here than it was in the backyard, no lush trees to shade the sunlight. I lean against the wooden banister and turn back toward the house.

"You were cheating on my sister."

"What?" His mouth hangs open for several seconds, waiting for me to supply more information. When I don't, he continues, "Look, Sienna. I know you're angry with Mattie. You're angry no one told you. But our relationship didn't start until months after Samantha died."

I'm sick and tired of the way people stress the word *months*. As though, even if this new relationship were totally above board, Colby and Matilda did their due diligence by waiting a decent amount of time before screwing, when even that time-line is pretty quick. After hearing what Harper saw on the Fourth of July, I know he began betraying my sister long before her death.

"I know that's a lie," I tell him. "You started sleeping together before Samantha died, and Matilda lied straight to my face."

"Look, Mattie wanted to talk to you. She was honest." He folds his arms across his chest. "I think it's easier for you to be upset if you think things started before Sammie died, and that's why you are insisting on this. You can ask the rest of our friends. They were surprised when we started dating, too, but they knew Mattie and I loved Sammie. We never would have done anything to hurt her."

There are several things I dislike about Colby, but at the top of that list is the patronizing way he talks to others. As though he's so much smarter, so convincing. The rest of the world just needs someone like him to come along and make sense of every-thing. It makes the fact I have two testaments of proof against him more satisfying.

"I know about the Fourth of July."

His reaction breaks, but only for a second. His pupils enlarge slightly. His lower lip trembles. Guys like Colby rehearse what they're going to say, all possible rebuttals and counterclaims, but they never are prepared to be called out on their own misdoings. They never expect the other person to have proof.

"What about July?"

"Someone saw you kissing Matilda. Not only was Samantha still alive, but she was also very much your girlfriend."

He opens his mouth and closes it. A smile breaks across his face as he turns his body away from me, hands on hips. It's amazing how quickly his calm demeanor has disintegrated into fidgeting and pacing. The opportunity to watch him squirm is even more gratifying than I'd imagined.

"Now, you're just making stuff up," he says at last. "You're lying."

"I'm not. And you know it."

For a few more seconds, he remains quiet. It looks as though he's struggling with coming up with another lie or falling back on the truth.

"Who told you that?"

"Does it matter?"

He's quiet, thinking. I believe if I cracked his head open at this precise moment, I'd be able to see the cogs and wires of his brain working in overtime. He sighs before facing me again. "Mattie and I did kiss on the Fourth of July, but it was a drunken mistake. That's it."

"Come on, Colby."

"I'm serious! Everyone at that party was wasted, and we both felt horrible afterward for betraying Sammie like that."

"Did you tell her what you'd done?"

"No! I mean, maybe a better man would have come clean, but it was a mistake. One mistake out of eight years together."

I find it hard to believe that in that length of time Colby only had one indiscretion. An indiscretion with my sister's friend that happened only a few months before she died.

"Who told you?" he asks again, this time his voice more serious.

Maybe I should tell him Harper was the one to let it slip. I might get to the truth faster if they start turning on one another, but I'm also afraid if they start bickering, they'll each get in their cars and drive away. I may never get another opportunity with them all together to find out what happened.

"Samantha thought you were cheating on her," I say, refocusing the conversation back to him.

Another shocked look. He even takes a step back, like my words have messed with his balance. "What? No, she didn't."

"She did. I have proof."

"Proof? Samantha's been dead for a year, and the two of you barely spoke around the time she died," he says. The way he says this last part turns my stomach, the way he uses our lack of communication as a weapon against me. "What possible proof could you have?"

It's time for me to use my only weapon—a weapon Samantha gave me—against them.

"I have her journal."

TWENTY-SEVEN

I walk back inside the cabin. Everyone is sitting in the living room like the ensemble cast of a sitcom. Upon seeing me, they each turn in different directions. Clearly, they were eavesdropping on our conversation. Or at least trying to.

"What do you mean you have her journal?" Colby says, following me inside.

I look at him briefly. His cheeks are red, his fingers clenching into a fist. Is that a line of sweat around his collar?

I ignore him and everyone else, moving quickly towards my bedroom. Once inside, I shut the door and lean against it.

I take a deep breath and close my eyes. That wasn't exactly how I wanted the conversation to go. Then again, I'm not sure what I was expecting. It's not like any of them were going to admit to wrongdoing without having evidence against them. I was just trying to catch them in lies before hitting them with the truth: I know all their secrets because of the journal.

Of course, none of them know what's inside it, but they must be wondering. They must be nervous. I know I wouldn't want my secrets to dangle over my head. It's a feeling of helplessness I'd do anything to avoid. Could one of them have killed to keep his or her secrets? Would they kill to take back that control?

A fist knocks against the door, making me jump.

"Go away, Colby!" I shout, after I've caught my breath.

"It's me," Jackson says, his voice a harsh whisper.

I let him inside, immediately leaning against the door again once it is closed, as though my small frame would be enough to keep someone from getting in.

"What the hell happened out there?"

"I confronted Colby."

"About what exactly?"

"Harper told me she caught Colby and Matilda kissing in July. Before Samantha died."

Jackson's thin lips morph into a perfect circle. "You're kidding."

"I told him about it, but I didn't say who told me."

"Well, it won't take him long to find out. You were clearly outside talking with Harper before you came in yelling."

"That's true," I said, having not thought about how easy it would be to piece it together. I'm too angry to be thinking straight. "Anyway, that means Matilda lied to my face last night when she promised nothing happened until *after* Samantha died. Knowing Colby, he probably put her up to it."

"So, he admitted to the affair?"

"Not exactly," I answer, honestly. "He admitted to the kiss. Said it was a mistake that happened once and then never again, until a few months ago. But how am I to believe him? He's doing what most people do when they've been caught. Admitting to one small part of a much bigger truth."

"Is that why he was so angry? You should see him out there. He's absolutely fuming."

"He wasn't angry when I called him out about the kiss. He was shocked, apologetic. He didn't get upset until I told him about the journal."

"You didn't."

"One of them knows more about Samantha's death than they're letting on," I say, moving away from the door to sit on the bed. "And what's in that diary proves that every single one of them has a motive to want Samantha out of the way."

"I'm guessing you're still not going to tell me what she said about the others?"

"Sure, I am," I say, reaching my hand beneath the mattress to pull out the diary. "I'm going to tell everyone right now."

"Are you sure that's the best idea?"

"Now that Colby knows I have it, the secret's out. He's probably telling them about it as we speak," I say. "He didn't seem happy to know Samantha had written about him in her diary."

A sound from the hallway interrupts our conversation. I stand, slowly, and we both look at the door. No one is pulling on the handle, pushing their way inside. Someone is just standing there. Listening.

For a moment, I think I'm paranoid, then I hear footsteps. There's a two-inch gap between the wooden floors and the bottom of the door. I spy two even shadows. Feet. Someone is listening to us. How long have they been there? What are they hoping to hear?

"Do you see that?" Jackson whispers to me, pointing at the door. I nod. He takes another breath before shouting at the closed door. "Hey, if you'd like to join the conversation, you're more than welcome!"

The shadows remain beneath the door another few seconds before slowly walking away.

"That was weird," Jackson says. "Someone must want to know what we're talking about."

I move toward the door, gripping the diary. "They're about to find out everything Samantha had to say about them."

TWENTY-EIGHT

Jackson and I don't leave the room right away. We spend another few minutes going over what I should say, how he should react if any of the others gets too angry. I'm grateful for an ally, especially when it feels like I'm trying to take down a wall built of secrets.

Then again, when I think back to the various details in Samantha's diary, maybe their friendships aren't as strong as they would like me, and the rest of the world, to believe. Sure, they've been a tight-knit group since college. They launched a successful company and continue to work alongside one another. But there are cracks in the foundation of their friendships, some I've witnessed in my short time here.

There's the outrage Harper, Nessa and Jackson all admitted to feeling when they first learned about Colby and Matilda's relationship. And there's the resentment Nessa feels, being the brains behind the company, and yet sharing the wealth with her inferior friends. Harper openly admitted to disliking Matilda, a sentiment that was reiterated again and again in Samantha's journal. Don't even get me started on Colby and Matilda. If they were willing to betray Samantha—his long-term girlfriend, her mentor and friend—then how loyal can they really be to the rest of the group?

Yes, they might put on a façade of close loyalty and friendship, but I have the advantage of knowing their weak points, and those are precisely where I'll aim my attacks.

"You ready?" Jackson asks, his hand already on the doorknob of my bedroom.

I nod, following him down the narrow hallway which leads to the elaborate living room. It's empty, and I feel a quick surge of rage at the thought the rest have taken their secrets and run. Then, I hear voices, muffled but near. To my left, I peer through the sliding glass door to see them all outside on the back balcony. Colby, Matilda, Harper and Nessa, all in deep conversation.

Jackson walks outside first, lowering his head to light a pre-rolled cigarette. I follow behind him. The quartet ends their conversation abruptly.

"Can we talk?" I begin.

Nessa takes a step forward. "You have Samantha's journal?"

"I didn't even know she kept a journal," Harper adds.

"That's why she wants to have a conversation," Jackson says.

"Is this why you invited her?" Harper asks, angrily. "Were you wanting to ambush us like this?"

"I assumed he wanted to out the fact I was dating Mattie," Colby says, his eyes scanning from Matilda to Jackson. "As usual, Jackson had other plans."

"What's that supposed to mean?" he asks.

"You always have something up your sleeve," Colby continues. "And now you've brought Sammie's sister here to confront us. Why? To prove you were somehow closer to her than the rest of us?"

"What is it you're trying to prove anyway?" Nessa asks, her eyes back on me.

Already, so many accusations and digs have been slung, it feels like my head is spinning. I'm outnumbered here. That much is obvious. I need to maintain what little control I have. I inhale slowly and deeply.

"I'm going inside," I say. "When you all are ready to talk, feel free to join me."

I refrain from looking at the others as I leave. Once inside, I sit in the burgundy armchair closest to the fireplace, put the journal on my lap, an ominous presence for the others whenever they decide to join me, and I wait.

Unsurprisingly, Jackson comes in first, after a few more raised voices transcend the walls.

"Why are they angry with you?" I ask him.

"I guess they heard us talking in your bedroom," he says, sitting in the center of the sofa across from me. "They're convinced I'm teaming up with you against them."

"You kind of are."

"I'm on the side of the truth. If there's more to Sammie's death, I want to know about it."

I think of the shadows we saw from beneath the doorway. Someone was listening to us, someone who reported back to the others, trying to stir controversy. Let them be upset. They don't have a choice but to do things my way, now that they know their own secrets are on the line.

Nessa enters the room next, her arms folded across her chest. She marches into the kitchen and takes one of the high-top barstools by the island, putting as much distance between us as possible. She won't even look in our direction.

Then Harper comes inside, sitting beside Jackson on the sofa. Another few minutes pass before Colby and Matilda join us. The couple remain standing at the back of the room.

"Okay, Sienna. You want to talk. Why don't you tell us what you came here to find out?"

"I came here because Jackson invited me," I say. "He said

this weekend was meant to memorialize my sister. There wasn't any other ulterior motive coming from him."

Jackson nods his thanks but remains silent.

"But you did have other reasons?" Harper asks.

"Not at first. In fact, I turned him down. I'm not particularly close with any of you. I've been mourning my sister every day for the past year. I didn't need some fancy trip to the mountains to miss her. And in the past year, I've had a lot of questions about her death. It just didn't make sense to me, the way it happened." I pause and hold up the diary. "But then I found this, and decided it was time I get to know the five of you better."

"You do know us," Nessa says. "You've known us for years."

"We've met each other, but you were in my sister's life, not mine."

"What is it you want to know?" Mattie asks.

"For starters, what was going on in Samantha's life in the weeks before she died?"

Heads raise, all of them looking at another, but no one says anything. Finally, Colby shrugs and says, "You're going to have to be more specific."

"Okay, well, you were living with her. Why weren't you at the condo that night?"

Colby shifts awkwardly in his seat. "Sammie made plans to visit your parents. It was a last-minute decision. I decided to visit some other friends that weekend, too. I never knew she came back to the condo," he says. "I didn't know until the next morning, when I found her."

I swallow hard, trying to fight away images of my sister lying helpless on the concrete. Dying alone. *I need you. Now.*

"Who were the friends?"

"Guys from college," he says, defensively. "You wouldn't know them. Believe it or not, I associate with people outside this group."

"Okay," I say, clearing my throat. "Where were the rest of you?"

Again, they swap glances, deciding who should go next. There's an air of intimidation in the room, and it can't be from my presence alone.

"I was at the office working late that weekend," Mattie says. "I had some projects I wanted to pitch later in the week. It was probably after midnight before I left."

"Do you live alone?"

"Yes, I do," she says, dryly. "It may not be much of an alibi, but it's the truth."

I look at Harper, waiting.

"Nessa and I were together that weekend," she says. "Since most of the gang was leaving town, we decided to have our own trip."

"We went to the hot springs and rented a room for the weekend," Nessa confirms.

"And you were there all weekend?"

"Yes," Harper says, hatefully. "And before you ask, none of us reached out to Samantha because we knew she was visiting your parents. None of us knew she decided to come back early."

"What about Jackson?" Matilda pipes up. "You never asked where he was?"

Jackson looks at me, then back at the others with disdain. Everyone is being accused of something here, but he appears the most offended.

"As we've already established, everyone was off doing their own thing that weekend. I visited my favorite local haunts. Even found a female companion for the night." He holds up his phone. "I didn't catch her name, but I'm sure her number is in here if I scroll back far enough."

"Pig," Harper says, under her breath.

That's one thing about Jackson, it may not be pretty, but it's the truth. At least, I hope it is.

"Anyway, if none of you have any more questions for me, do you think we could move on?"

"Yes, please. Let's get to the journal," Colby says. "I don't like the way you're waving that thing around like it's some axe over our heads."

And yet, that's exactly what it is, and every person in this room knows it.

TWENTY-NINE

I hold each person's gaze as I open the journal, dramatically flipping through the pages.

"Samantha had some interesting things to say about all of you. No surprise there. After all, the six of you have been inseparable since your college days. Given what she had to say, I can't help wondering if one of you had a motive to want her dead."

"You're accusing us of *killing* her?" Matilda asks, outraged.

Even that accusation seems strong. There isn't enough to lead to that conclusion. Yet. But I think all of them are holding something back.

"I think you all know more about Samantha's death than you are saying," I say, at last. "And from what I've read in that journal, you're all skilled liars."

"Okay, I don't know what you're getting at with the rest of them, but I have nothing to hide," Nessa says, her arms still crossed. In fact, she looks as though she has barely moved since she entered the room.

"Are you sure about that?" Jackson comes to my defense.

"She said the five of us," Harper says. "That means she has dirt on you, too."

"Fine. I'll go first." Jackson stands, turning his back to me so that he can face the others. "I was in love with Samantha. I broke down and told her a few months before she died and she turned me down. Happy now?"

I study each of their reactions closely. Matilda looks down at the floor. Colby stares at Jackson, his jaw clenched. Harper looks behind her and locks eyes with Nessa. They seem to be the only two in the room who aren't surprised by the admission.

"And you found this out by reading it in Sammie's journal?" Colby asks me.

"Yes."

"I'll do the rest of the work for you," Jackson says. "Sienna has already told us the journal holds a potential motive for each of us to want her sister dead. I'm guessing this one was mine. I was in love with a girl who had strictly friend-zoned me. To some people, that might be a reason to kill, but I would never hurt Sammie."

"You are a total asshole," Colby says.

"I understand she was dating you at the time, but like I said, she turned me down. That should make you happy."

"You're an asshole because you've given Matilda and I nothing but hell since we got together, all while you were pining after my girlfriend."

"Wow. That wasn't the reaction I was expecting," Harper says. "Way to make it about you."

"Oh, shut it," Colby spits.

"Is that everything she said about Jackson?" Harper asks, turning her attention back to me.

Jackson turns to look at me, waiting. I kept my promise not to tell him what was written about the others. He must wonder if I've withheld info about him, too.

I look into my lap, finding it too painful to meet his eyes. "Everything Jackson said is true. She also talked about his substance abuse. She worried he would get carried away at times. That his behavior might reflect poorly on the business." I force myself to look at Jackson. "But mostly she was just worried about you."

He nods slowly before facing the group and raising his hands at his sides. "See? Not so bad to be honest, is it? Nessa, you still maintain you have nothing to hide?"

Nessa ignores him, looking at me instead. "What did she write about me?"

"She said you misused company funds." Suddenly, I'm squirming. I'm not used to wielding this amount of power over other people, and even though I'm convinced outing their secrets will lead to answers, I'm struck by the feeling I'm in over my head. "She said you've been lying about your credentials for years. Even back in college. She said you plagiarized your thesis."

"That's bullshit," Harper says, standing.

"You're making this up," Colby adds, equally enraged. "Sammie would never accuse Nessa of something like that, let alone put it in writing."

Nessa's silence at the back of the room becomes deafening. Everyone turns to face her.

"Nessa, don't you have anything to say?" Matilda asks.

Still sitting on the barstool, Nessa's foot begins tapping on the floor. Her cheeks are a deep purple.

"It's not like how she's making it sound," she says at last.

Colby takes a step closer to her. "Nessa?"

"It's hard to find a footing in this industry. We all know that. Especially for me. I don't have the financial support from family the rest of you have. I had to jump through a few loopholes in order to get the funding we needed."

"What did you do?" Jackson asks, suddenly invested in her answer.

"I did what needed to be done in order to secure funding."

"Was it legal?" Harper asks.

Silence. Then finally, Nessa says, "Nothing can come back on us. I made sure of that."

"Oh my gosh." Matilda sits down on one of the chairs by the dining room table.

"And Sammie knew about this?" Colby asks.

"She confronted me about it," she says. "Before the spring launch party. One of our accountants found a discrepancy and brought it to her for review. She did some digging, and found out what I had done."

"You put the business in jeopardy?" Jackson says. "Our livelihood?"

"Don't make it sound so dramatic," Nessa says, shifting in her seat. "Like I said, I did what needed to be done, and it's over."

"You've broken trust, Nessa," Colby says. "How do we know you wouldn't do something like that again if you found yourself in a tight situation?"

"It won't happen again," Nessa says firmly. "I only did it once."

"What about in college," Harper says. "Is it true you plagiarized your thesis?"

Nessa stands. "You don't get it. There were a dozen other people up for the post-graduate grant, but I needed it more than them. The others that missed out still found funding. They could just ask their parents. I didn't have that option. The only way I could ensure I'd get a head start was to take it myself, so that's what I did."

Everyone's body language has shifted. Even Harper refuses to look at her friend. Her posture mimics Nessa's from only moments ago. Arms crossed, closed off from the rest of the room. Nessa was supposed to be the stable one of the group, the person they could all trust. To learn she'd lied about the business—had been lying since her college days...

And if Samantha knew all this, it provides one hell of a motive.

The others see it, too. Nessa's secret is far bigger than some unrequited crush.

"What did she say about me?" Harper asks. "I want to know."

"She said you weren't pulling your weight," I say. "Samantha and some of the others had talked about letting you go."

Harper looks around at the others. "Is that true? Were you trying to kick me out of my own company?"

"Sammie and I were the only founding members," Nessa says, under her breath.

"And what's that make the rest of us?" Jackson quips. "Our work the past four years means nothing because it was your idea?"

"I didn't say that—"

"Who wanted me out?" Harper cuts off the argument between Nessa and Jackson before it can start. She's staring at me, now as desperate for answers as I am.

"The journal didn't say."

"All right then." Harper stands too, facing the others. "Which one of you talked to her about booting me out?"

"I did," Colby says, firmly. "The only reason you still had a job was because you were Samantha's oldest friend, but I told her we'd never get ahead if we based our department chairs on charity."

"Charity?" The anger in Harper's voice is gone, replaced with something else. "I've given everything to this company."

"Sometimes that's still not enough," Colby says. "Nessa and Sammie were the brains behind the company. Jackson did his part for marketing. Mattie runs our social media. I'm in charge of finance. What did you do besides walk around the office and make yourself look busy?"

"That's a little low," Matilda says, her voice so quiet I almost don't catch it.

"It's true," Colby insists. "That's the exact conversation I had with Sammie before she died."

"Okay, Mr. Finance. Maybe if you'd been more concerned with your own responsibilities you would have caught Nessa's mistake instead of some entry level accountant."

"Maybe you're right," he says. "But you wanted to know who talked to Sammie, and I'm telling you."

"Did she say anything else?" Harper asks, her watery eyes back on me.

"She said you had it out for Matilda."

"What?" Mattie speaks up.

"Apparently the way Colby felt about Harper is the way Harper felt about you."

"Sure, I'll admit it," Harper says. "You don't bring anything new or unique to the company. You're only around because you're friends with Sammie."

"That's not true," Colby says, stepping up to defend his girlfriend.

"You literally just said the same things about me."

"Okay, so both Harper and Mattie were at risk of getting fired," Nessa interjects. "Anything else we need to know?"

"She said Matilda was copying her every move," I say, looking at her. "She was afraid you might poach the company's clients if you decided to start your own business."

"What about me?" Harper asks.

"She worried you knew something you weren't telling her."

"Well, that one's easy." Harper stands, pointing at Colby and Matilda. "I'm the one who caught you two kissing on the Fourth of July."

Nessa's jaw drops. Jackson stares at the couple, something like hate in his eyes.

"That was a one-time mistake," Colby says, tensely.

"It was," Matilda chimes in. "We both felt terrible about it. Especially after..." she struggles, "after Sammie died so suddenly."

"Isn't it convenient that the two of you cheated on her when Sammie was alive," Nessa says, "and now you're a couple."

"It's not a good look, I understand that," Colby says. "It was a drunken mistake. A kiss. Nothing else started until we were both grieving Sammie."

"Yeah, stick to your story," Harper says, crossing her arms. "If I could go back, my reaction would have been different. I'll always regret not telling her."

Another wave of silence washes over the room. It's as though the release of everyone's secrets has taken everyone's energy with them.

"That only leaves Colby," Jackson says. "What did she say about him?"

I look at Colby, making sure to maintain eye contact. "She thought he was cheating on her."

If it's possible for a silence to become even quieter, it just did.

"I wasn't," Colby says.

Matilda turns her head, letting her hair fall to conceal her face.

"So, there we have it," Jackson says. "One person committed fraud to help the company. Two people were at risk of losing their jobs. I was in love with Samantha, and Colby was a cheater. At least, that's how Samantha viewed each of us."

"That's right," I say. "It's all in her journal."

"That's five possible motives." Jackson, again.

"Or maybe we're all just complicated people," Matilda says, "and Sammie's death was still an accident."

"Did she write anything else?" Colby asks, and I get the strange feeling that he was expecting another revelation that hasn't yet been mentioned.

"No." I thumb through the pages. "There were pages ripped from the back of the journal. There's no way of knowing what they said."

Is it just me, or does a wave of relief seem to pass through the room? It's as though they were all afraid of hearing something else.

"Okay, then. I think it's time for another smoke," Jackson says, walking toward the sliding glass doors.

"I'll join you," Nessa says. "I could use some fresh air."

That leaves Harper, Colby, Matilda and me alone in the room. Neither of us want to speak anymore, but I believe we're all too wiped to go anywhere.

"You really think one of us would hurt your sister?" Mattie says.

"I don't know. I think there's a lot about her death that doesn't make sense. I thought one of these secrets might lead somewhere."

"Like Mattie said, we're complicated people," Colby says. "That doesn't make us murderers. These secrets you bring up... they were all ongoing issues, problems we were addressing. None of it was motive for one of us to harm Sammie."

I look away from him, contemplating what he said. There's some truth there. Relationships are complicated, a never-ending carousel of highs and lows. I've pointed out their low points, their weaknesses, but is any of it enough?

"We all loved Sammie," Harper says. "And I know you did, too, which is why you're so desperate to make sense of her death. But hashing out our secrets and turning us against one another won't bring you closure."

"I know, but I—"

I'm interrupted by a loud cry from outside. Someone is screaming from the back deck.

THIRTY

The four of us take off running toward the sliding glass door just as another scream rings out.

"No! Oh my gosh!" Nessa shouts.

"What happened?" Matilda is the first one to reach her.

Nessa is standing by the door, covering her mouth with her hands.

"Where's Jackson?" I ask, my eyes scanning the rest of the empty deck.

Nessa raises her hand and points at the railing. "He was right there when he fell."

"Fell?" Colby charges toward the railing.

I follow him, afraid to look down. There's easily a six-foot drop between the second-floor balcony and the ground beneath. I search the area, seeing nothing but overgrown vegetation and fallen green leaves. A wave of vertigo almost sends me to my knees.

This is exactly what happened to Samantha.

This is how she died.

"Jackson?" Colby cups his hands around his mouth to try and increase his volume.

The only sounds we hear are the clicking of branches and twittering of birds.

"Right here," Harper says. She's standing a few steps away from us, pointing down.

We rush over to her and look below. There's still lush greenery everywhere, but beneath that, I see a protruding leg, still and pale.

"Jackson!" I shout. My heart has jumped into my throat.

Our raised voices are carried into the woods, through the wilderness. Then we hear a low mumbling sound.

"Oh, my goodness, Jackson? Are you okay?"

He doesn't answer, but the sounds are unmistakably human, full of pain.

"I'm going to run around to the front, see if I can climb down to where he is," Colby says.

Without thinking, I follow, catching the tail end of a conversation before I disappear inside.

"What happened?" Harper asks.

"He was leaning against the railing," Nessa answers, "then he fell—"

I can't worry about what happened before he fell, only what's happening now. We have to get to Jackson, make sure he's okay. Colby and I rush through the front door and cut left; to reach Jackson, we must traverse the unmanicured side of the house, the side still overtaken by wilderness. There's a steep embankment rounding the house. It doesn't look safe to cross, and yet it's the only way to reach him.

"Balance yourself on the trees," Colby says. Whether he's talking to himself or to me, I'm not sure. "We don't need another fall."

The trees beside the house are scrawny and tall. I lean against one before shifting my balance to another as I make my way along the uneven terrain. I try not to think about what could be around me, camouflaged in the earth—spiders and snakes and insects. We've almost made it to flat land because I can see a small air conditioning unit resting beside the cabin's foundations.

"Jackson, can you hear us?" Colby shouts.

We're moving toward the general direction of the back porch, but it's still difficult to navigate. Everything looks the same, green and busy. When we look ahead, we see trunk-like beams holding the cabin in place.

I hear faint moaning. "Keep going," I say.

When we find Jackson, he's inverted, having landed on the upper half of his body, his left leg caught in the high branches of a bramble bush. It looks to have broken his fall, although the tiny thorns have torn at his skin. Streaks of blood trickle down his calves.

"Can you see him?" Matilda's voice rings out from over-head, might as well be an angel calling from the heavens.

"He's right here," Colby shouts back. He lowers his voice. "Jackson, can you hear us?"

"Hmmph."

Jackson acknowledges us, but he's in so much pain, it seems impossible for him to form words. I push back the branches and leaves around his body. His leg is bent awkwardly, clearly broken. My own bones ache and my stomach roils at the sight of it.

"This isn't good," Colby says.

"Do we need to call an ambulance?" Harper cries.

"I don't know," Colby says, evaluating Jackson's broken body. "He needs help but there's no telling how long it could take an ambulance to get here."

"I can't get service!" Matilda yells, already trying to signal help.

"We'd probably get there faster if we drove him ourselves," Colby says to me.

"We don't know where the nearest hospital is," I say.

Jackson moans again. "I don't know if we can even carry him back up the hill."

"Use the house phone," Colby shouts. "Call the cabin owner. He can give us directions."

"I'm doing it now," Harper says. Moments later, I hear footsteps stomping on the planked porch overhead, rushing inside the house.

"Jackson, we're going to try and move you," Colby says.

Jackson only mumbles something in reply. Gratitude or hesitation, I'm not sure. Colby moves around so that both his hands are on Jackson's shoulder blades, and he begins to push.

Jackson lets out a painful yelp.

"This is bad," I say, under my breath.

"We have to do something. We can't just leave him here until help comes. Bend down and let him lean on you for stabilization. Once he gets on his feet, we can help him up the hill to the front of the house."

I nod and get in position, kneeling in front of Jackson. I squeeze his hands. "You're going to be okay," I say. "Just lean on me."

I think Jackson nods his understanding, but he's so out of it, I can't be sure. His head lolls to the side.

"One. Two. Three."

Colby begins pushing and Jackson continues to cry out. I stay motionless, allowing him to lean on me for support, feeling the full weight of him, while also trying to hold tight to his broken leg. Soon Jackson is upright, his back leaning against the same tree that broke his fall.

"Okay, it might take some time, but we need to walk him up the hill. You get one side, I'll get the other."

"What about his leg?"

"I'll hold the bulk of his weight. Try to move the leg as little as possible."

It feels like an impossible feat. Navigating the small drop off was hard enough for just myself. I'm afraid of losing my grip and Jackson falling, injuring himself even more.

But we don't have many options. If we want to get him help, we first need to get him to the main road.

"Lean on me," I tell Jackson. "We'll be out of here before you know it."

THIRTY-ONE

TROY

Troy slams the door so hard, the entire cab of his truck shakes.

It's only a ten-minute drive from his trailer to the cabin, but each passing second feels like it's bringing him closer to disaster. In some ways, Troy always feels this way, but he tries to deny that feeling, that fear, like someone with a fever denying he is sick.

When he got the call from the girl—he's not even sure if it was the nerdy girl with the book or the blonde with hair down to her waist—she sounded hysterical; he couldn't make out what she was saying. After telling her to slow down, he gathered the details he needed to know.

Falling.

Balcony.

Broken bones.

The girl asked if they should call an ambulance, but that would only waste precious time. Response times in this area are horrible. Back when he was in high school, he remembered a classmate getting injured in gym class. It had taken the ambulance forty-five minutes to reach the campus, and those were mostly straight roads.

These winding mountain roads, half of which are still made of gravel, could make it more than an hour before help arrived. It's not something he likes to flag to his renters, but it's true. Whereas, if he gets there himself, he can be back down the mountain and at Smoky Mountain Memorial in fifteen minutes flat.

He just hopes whatever happened, the person isn't too seriously injured.

Troy knew there was something off about this group. Could feel it from the moment they pulled up to the cabin in that shiny BMW. How does someone even fall off a balcony? He's always looking after the place, making sure everything is safe and maintained. The guy must have been doing something reckless. Trying to climb it or leaning over too far. That's the only thing that could explain it.

On second thought, after watching the way the group interacted with each other on that first day, maybe he was pushed.

When Troy pulls up to the cabin, all the renters are waiting on the porch out front. Lying on the gravel in front of the house is the blond-haired guy from yesterday. Troy could have guessed he'd be the one to get hurt.

"What happened?" Troy asks, walking over to them.

"He fell off the back balcony," one of them answers. He's not sure which one.

"How the hell did you get him up here?"

"We carried him up," the girl with black hair says. Sienna, he remembers. She's hunched over, hands on her knees, like she's out of breath from the climb.

"Did you call an ambulance?" the other guy asks.

"It'll be faster if we give him a ride. The closest hospital is fifteen minutes away," he says. "I'll drive."

"I'll help you get him in the truck," the guy says. Colby, Troy remembers now. The one who took so long getting up here yesterday.

Troy and Colby help a broken Jackson into the back seat of the quad cab. They lay him flat, propping his wounded leg on a pile of tarp Troy had stored in the truck bed.

"I'm going with you," Sienna says, climbing into the passenger seat.

"Fine by me," Troy says, walking around to the driver's side.

"Are you sure about that?" Colby asks Sienna, his voice suddenly low and protective.

Troy didn't like the tone of Colby's voice, insinuating she might be in danger just because he had a Southern accent, and some dusted up boots. He was trying to help these people, but even that didn't stop them from treating him like *the* help.

"I'll be fine," she says, fastening her seat belt. "Let you know when I hear something."

"We love you, Jackson," the blonde girl shouts from the porch, even though the guy in the back can't hear her. He's in another world of pain, needs medication immediately. The other two girls are on either side of her, watching the entire scene in wide-eyed, nail-bitten silence. Colby remains standing by the truck. He doesn't move even after Troy begins to pull away. There's something in Colby's stare Troy doesn't like. Anger. Mistrust.

"You said fifteen minutes, right?" Sienna asks.

"Yep."

Troy turns his eyes back to the road, tries to shake off the bad feeling the guy in the rearview mirror gives him. You'd think he'd be more worried about his friend with the broken limb than Troy, who was going above and beyond on his day off to help. But that's how guys like Colby were. Convinced they knew best but never really wanting to do anything themselves.

At least Troy knew how to keep his loved ones safe.

Then, with a shudder, he remembered, and realized that wasn't always true.

THIRTY-TWO

SIENNA

I'm staring through the open blinds on the window of Jackson's recovery room. He's covered in blankets, his leg propped up into a sling. The doctors said he'll be under sedation for the next couple of hours, but other than the severe fracture on his right leg, there doesn't appear to be any further damage. He's going to be okay.

I lean forward, resting my forehead on the glass. We've been here for hours, the increasing time causing a giant headache. There was a rush to get him into the ER, and then several annoying exchanges with the nursing staff over his condition. I didn't have any of his medical insurance cards or information. In the rush to get here, I didn't think to grab his wallet. But he's resting now. That's all that matters.

"Did the doctors say anything else?"

The cabin owner stands behind me, both his hands tucked into his front pockets.

"Just that he needs rest. He'll be here the rest of the week-end, if not longer." I press two fingers against my eyes, trying to wipe away the exhaustion. "You didn't have to wait with me."

"It's fine," he says. "Didn't have anything else planned for the day."

"I guess we can head back to the cabin. Now that I know the way, I can tell the others how to get here if we need to come back."

As we exit the hospital, I feel guilty. The fall could have been much worse, and I should be happy that Jackson is okay, but I can't shake the feeling I'm leaving a soldier behind as I make the bumpy ride back up the mountain.

"You need anything from town before we head back?" he asks, fastening his seat belt.

"What's your name?"

"Troy."

"I'm Sienna."

"I remember from yesterday," he says. "Pretty name."

"Sorry I forgot yours. A lot has happened since we arrived."

And the idea of returning to the cabin without Jackson makes me nauseous. He was the only person I thought I could trust, my ally. I was able to confront all of Samantha's friends with their secrets, but that drama was interrupted by the fall. There's no telling what the mood will be once I return.

"You ever been here before?"

"I haven't. I think some of the others have. They always travel together."

"You're not part of that group?"

"Not really."

Troy keeps his eyes on the road, as we merge off the highway. "You look familiar. I thought maybe I'd rented to you before."

"Nope. First time. And last, if I'm being honest."

"Your friend is lucky," Troy says. "That fall could have been a lot worse. There are some balconies with a much higher drop."

I don't want to think about it, all the dangerous drops a person could encounter. Samantha's fall wasn't that far, but unlike Jackson, there were no bushes and trees to break it. Only concrete rested beneath her balcony. I imagine the setting, imagine Samantha's body breaking hard against the ground, her blood staining the cement. Troy is right. Jackson was lucky.

"I'm happy he's going to be okay."

"You have any idea how he fell? I mean, I inspect the place between visits. The railing is high enough he shouldn't have been able to topple over."

"I wasn't outside when it happened."

The only person who was with him was Nessa, and even she seemed unsure. For a moment, I wonder if she could have done something to Jackson. Tensions were at their highest right before he fell. I'd just accused her of cheating her way through college and stealing from the company, but they were only out there a few minutes before we heard the scream, and she seemed genuinely shaken about the accident.

"Y'all are here for some kind of memorial?"

I get the feeling Troy doesn't spend a lot of time around other people. Not surprising, considering he lives and works in the middle of nowhere. He's spent the entire Saturday afternoon sitting with me at the hospital and I couldn't even remember his name. The least I could do is humor him with conversation.

"My sister died last year."

There's a slight reaction, hands tightening around the wheel. He wasn't expecting my answer to be so personal.

"I'm sorry. That's got to be tough."

"Yeah. It is." Maybe it's my exhaustion after a long day, or the fact that I'm alone with someone who isn't tied to Samantha, but I feel comfortable talking. "The people on this trip were her closest friends. They started a business together. I'm kind of an outsider among them, really. Jackson was the one who invited me to come, and now he's stuck in the hospital."

There's a silence as the truck climbs the side of the moun-

tain. It feels nice to talk with someone, but I've been out of practice so long, small talk is hard. I sense the same energy coming
from Troy.

"My dad died a couple years ago," he says, at last. "It doesn't
get any easier."

"I'm sorry."

"Did you hear about the wildfires that tore through here a
few years back?"

I shake my head.

"It broke out in the fall. Still aren't sure how it happened,
really. But you get the right amount of wind and little rain, and
the fires can just take over. It damaged over a hundred acres of
property. Ruined several homes on the other side of the mountain. Several businesses ended up shutting down, and never
opened back up. Eight people died."

"That is awful."

I feel guilty, realizing an event was so devastating for a
whole community and I knew nothing about it. I feel even
worse thinking of how the others mocked Troy for his strict
rules and procedures; it's obvious now he has them in place for a
reason.

"It was rough. Took me several years to get the business up
and running again. I own three cabins now, and I'm happy with
that amount. The fires ran for three or four days before a big
rain came through and snuffed them out. It's funny how something that lasts for such a short amount of time takes years to
recover from.

"Anyway, that's why I'm always pushing so hard when it
comes to safety. Most accidents come from human error, people
not taking things as seriously as they should."

"I can't speak for everyone in the group, but I try to be
cautious." I look out the car window. There's a small squirrel
running along the side of the road, its bushy tail bouncing with

every stride. "Honestly, now that Jackson's hurt, I wouldn't be surprised if we cut the trip short."

There's another pause. The sun is turning a bright orange. It's beautiful, the backdrop far different from anything I might expect to see back home.

"So, your sister. How old was she?"

"My age. We were twins."

He shifts in his seat again, and I begin to think the conversation is getting too personal. He regrets asking. After all, he went on about the wildfires and the people who died but didn't elaborate about his father's death.

"Well, I'm sorry for your loss. And I'm sorry the weekend hasn't turned out the way you wanted."

"Thanks."

The weekend certainly has turned into something different. Troy doesn't know anything about my real motives for being here. This trip was never about remembering my sister, at least for me. All I wanted to do was get answers about her death. Now that won't happen. Jackson's accident gives everyone an excuse to go their separate ways, and I'll never get a chance to confront them again.

We pull into the clearing in front of the cabin. Troy parks behind Colby's car.

"Thanks again for driving," I say. "We'll try to leave you alone the rest of the time we're here."

"No worries." He waves. "I'm happy to help."

I climb out of the car, making my way to the cabin. Troy remains in the parking lot a few more seconds, before he backs out to leave.

THIRTY-THREE

TROY

Troy makes a three-point turn to get his car back on the gravel road. His stomach feels like it's doing somersaults.

All that talk about death and dying didn't help. He tries not to think much about the wildfires, about how much was taken from the people around him when they broke out.

He tries not to think about his father.

But that's not why he suddenly feels sick to his stomach.

This group had given him a bad feeling from the start. A familiar feeling. That sensation got worse when he had to rush one of the renters to the ER.

He feels sorry for Sienna, being stuck out here in the middle of nowhere with people that aren't even her friends. From the sounds of it, people she can't even trust.

And he knows they shouldn't be trusted either. None of it clicked until that last conversation, when Sienna mentioned her sister. A twin.

He thought he recognized Sienna on that first day, but he knows now they've never met before.

But her sister?

He remembers her well.

THIRTY-FOUR

SIENNA

The hairs on my arm stand at attention, the air conditioning inside the cabin on full blast. When I walk through the front door, I find the four remaining house guests gathered around the kitchen island. Bags full of chips and bowls full of dips are scattered around, a full wine glass in front of each of them.

"Sienna," Colby says. "Finally, you're back."

"Yeah." The word comes out deflated. When Jackson fell, I was riding on full adrenaline, but now exhaustion has taken over.

Harper stands from the barstool where she'd been sitting, Nessa behind her. "How is Jackson?"

"Admitted and under sedation. I'm hoping to hear something later this evening."

"What's the damage?" Nessa asks.

"Broken leg. Besides that, he's okay. Doctors said he was lucky."

"We tried calling you," Mattie said.

"You know reception on the mountain is shit, and everything was so hectic at the hospital."

"Sure. Right," Colby says. "Thank you for going with him."

"I'm surprised you all are still here," I say, sitting on the empty barstool. "Jackson's fall has pretty much ruined the weekend. I figured you'd use the opportunity to call it quits and head home."

"We needed to know he was okay first," Harper says.

"And we wanted to check in on you," Nessa adds.

I nod. Just before Jackson fell, tensions were at their highest. I'd confronted them with their secrets, openly accused them of having something to do with Samantha's death, then everything was interrupted with our race to the hospital. It makes sense they'd continue the conversation after I left.

"Where should we start?" I ask, feeling too exhausted to go back into battle.

"First, we want to apologize," Matilda begins, catching me by surprise. "We talked some things over, and I don't think any of us stopped to consider where you're coming from. In the past year, we've been able to lean on each other. You haven't had that. It's understandable you'd have questions about what was happening in Samantha's life leading up to her death."

An apology. I wasn't expecting that. Earlier there was arguing and yelling and finger pointing, all punctuated by Jackson's scream as he fell over the railing. Since before I even arrived, I believed it was me against the group. Samantha's sister at war with Samantha's friends.

"We understand how the journal might reopen new wounds," Nessa says. "It's been a year since Sammie died, then suddenly you find this journal that unloads all these secrets. You must feel a stronger connection to her since reading it."

Nessa's right. For months after Samantha died, I floated, waiting to hear her voice, the realization that that would never happen again refusing to cement itself in my mind. It was a different type of grief. Then, the journal. With her words and her handwriting and her sense of humor. In some ways, it felt like my sister had returned, was whispering her deepest secrets to me again, like she did when we were children. And I missed my sister so much, I was willing to take every word and accusation as gospel.

"None of us are perfect," Harper says. "There's some truth to everything that was written about us, but just because we have secrets and make mistakes doesn't mean any of us wanted to hurt Sammie."

"Your sister made all our lives better. Mine especially," Colby says. "Maybe we took her for granted, but you must believe us when we say none of us wanted her dead. All relationships, all friendships, have their lows, but we'd do anything to have her back."

"It's true," Matilda says.

And somewhere deep inside, I know it is. Is there any relationship in the world that hasn't been tested, either with annoyances or faults or outright betrayals? And they don't all end in tragedy or murder. No, it's far more likely that imperfect people find their way through those issues. It's what Samantha would have had to do to maintain friendships of a decade or more. It's a kind of loyalty I don't understand because the person who played the biggest role in my life was Samantha, and now she's gone.

From the moment I heard about Samantha's fall, I've been searching for more. Something that will make sense of her death, someone to blame. When I first started throwing around accusations, I remember the way my parents begged me to let it go. The way the police looked at me. The pity on their faces. It may not be her friends' intention, but they're looking at me the same way right now. A lonely sister desperate to make sense of something that never will.

Is that what has been fueling this weekend? Desperation? Reading the diary convinced me to twist every detail for my own benefit, to paint my sister's friends in the most unflattering light. Now, they're admitting their faults, admitting their mistakes, but maintaining their love for my sister. They're even apologizing to me, after the horrible way I've treated them.

All of them are grieving, too, I must remember. Colby and Harper and Matilda and Nessa. Jackson. Poor Jackson, the most dramatic of the group, was quick to join my quest for revenge, and where did that lead him? The hospital. If things hadn't been so heated, would he have even fallen? My own agenda has put yet another person in danger and admitting that fact releases a sharp pain of regret in my chest.

"I'm sorry," I say, my hard exterior falling away. "You're right. I was just looking for a way to stay close to her."

"We understand that." Suddenly, Harper is behind me, her hand on my shoulder. "That's what this weekend was supposed to be about. A celebration of Samantha's life."

"And gratitude," Nessa adds. "For how she made all of our lives better."

"I just hate that Jackson isn't here with us," Matilda says. "He cared about her, too."

I picture him now, broken bones, pricked with IVs and meds. Now the sobs come, an unstoppable stream breaking through the barriers I've been so determined to build.

I cry for him.

I cry for Samantha.

I cry for the many situations I can't control and will never be able to change. Before I can lift my head, I feel arms around me. The three women hold me close, as I imagine they held my own sister in moments of despair.

"Let's just enjoy the rest of the weekend, yeah?" Colby says. "It didn't start off the way any of us wanted, but we can change that."

"For Samantha," I say, my voice still shaking with emotion.

It's always been easy for me to criticize Samantha's friends, to highlight their faults, but I have to remember that there were multiple reasons my sister kept these people in her life. Maybe it's time I push through my own judgements and biases and start looking at the world through her eyes.

It would be a far more beautiful world if I did.

THIRTY-FIVE

The rest of the group decides to gather around the firepit again. I join them at first, but my tiredness soon takes over. It's been a long day for all of us, but the countless time spent at the hospital stole hours I'll never get back. Not to mention the crying fit I had earlier. Rarely do I let down my walls, especially in front of people I hardly know. I'm absolutely wiped.

As I walk into the living room, I peer onto the back porch, the scene of this afternoon's crisis. Recalling the arguments from earlier makes me cringe.

Moving into the kitchen, I pour a glass of water. For the first time since this morning, I'm alone.

I never thought I'd say this, but my heart leaps with gratitude that the others didn't leave while I was at the hospital. Jackson's fall, combined with the accusations I was throwing around would have been too much for most. I feel guilty. I was never welcome here, not really. Samantha's closest friends planned this trip, and I turned it into my own personal vendetta.

And why? Because of a few entries written in my sister's journal. It's not like she only wrote about her friends. There were plenty of passages about boring day-to-day happenings, passages about her own hopes and dreams, which were never to be fulfilled.

Yet, I clung to those few paragraphs where she wrote about her friends' secrets, hoping it would somehow lead me to an understanding about my sister's death. Perhaps I was foolish to do that. Selfish, even. All of us have secrets, and I've chosen to make this trip about exposing the lives of the people closest to my sister. Maybe their faults were just that. Faults with no ulterior motives behind them. And now I've ruined this trip—ruined my sister's honor—with my paranoia and accusations.

Jackson's enthusiasm last night gave me hope. He knows Colby and the girls better than I do, was aware of their different dynamics. If he thought they had something to hide, maybe there was something to back up my suspicions. But again, there is some truth to what Colby said earlier, about Jackson always having something up his sleeve. Jackson can be dramatic. Maybe he was creating scenarios as freely as I was. Now that I know about his true feelings for Samantha, it makes sense. He regrets the time he spent with her because he spent much of it not being true to himself and his heart. He must think that if he said something sooner, maybe there would have been a chance at a relationship between them. Like me, Jackson is pining for a second chance at something that will never be.

I walk onto the back porch. The sun is starting to dip behind the mountains, a bright orange orb flattening into blue sky. I walk over to the balcony, near where Jackson took his ugly fall. I feel guilty for that too. Because of my paranoia, tension ran so high Jackson lost his balance. He could have been killed. My stomach does somersaults; I'm sickened to think my own craziness could have cost Jackson his life.

Perhaps it's time I regain control of this situation—regain control of my wild feelings—before it is too late.

A breeze makes a hushing sound in the leaves, raising chill

bumps on my arm. The mountains are colder at night. As I'm turning to go inside, something captures my attention. Something shiny and out of shape against the tawny deck below the railing. I bend down and pick it up.

A small nail. I look around, wondering where it might have come from. There are no tables and chairs on this side of the deck, no lanterns or lights hanging. I take a closer look at the railing itself.

The wooden pillars which make up the safety fence are loose, but it doesn't look like the damage happened accidentally, like during Jackson's fall, for instance. And it's not just one piece of wood, but several. Two, three, four. The planks have been intentionally loosened, as though someone wanted someone to lean against them and topple over the side.

I stare back at the screw in my hand, a heavy thumping beginning in my chest.

Maybe Jackson's fall wasn't an accident after all.

Their happy, drunken voices carry through the air, burning my ears. One of them must have deliberately loosened the screw. One of them must have wanted Jackson—or hell, maybe, even me—to fall. They needed the questions surrounding Samantha and the diary to end, and the plan almost worked. For a few hours, I believed I was imposing my own demands on everyone, seeing only what I wanted to see.

I roll the screw between my hands, feeling the cool, carved metal. My original vision returns to me. One of them has something to hide. Tomorrow, when everyone is sober and unassuming after our night of revelry, I plan on finding out which one.

THIRTY-SIX

TROY

Sundays are about family.

It's a message that's driven hard around these parts from a young age. Drive down any main street in town, and you'll see packs of people in their Sunday finery, looking for the best restaurant for their post-church meal.

Troy stopped going to church years ago, but he still has a strong relationship with God. He reads his Bible several times throughout the week, even prays when life starts to feel overwhelming. The main reason he stopped going to church is because his own family is so small, and despite the packed pews, a sanctuary can feel very lonely on your own.

Troy's new routine every Sunday morning is to snag an Early Riser's Special at his favorite diner. The waitress slaps the menu on the table. Troy takes it, feeling the sticky cleaning fluid from where it has just been wiped down.

"Thanks, Rosie," he says, discreetly wiping his hand with the napkin in his lap.

"You got it, honey. Happy you come to see me on the weekends," she says. She's wearing jeans and a sweater. You'd think she was a customer, but Troy knows better. He's known Rosie most of his life.

"Never feel like cooking on Sundays," he says.

Truthfully, Troy doesn't feel like being alone. He isn't sure what awakened his loneliness last night. Maybe it was the exhausting hours spent at the hospital with the renter who'd fallen off the balcony, his worry about being held liable for any damage caused. Or his short, but talkative car ride with Sienna. Either way, he wants to be around people. Families coming together for lunch after Sunday morning services. Tourists taking in one last meal before they make the drive home, to wherever that is.

More likely, Troy doesn't want to be alone after making the discovery that he has met Sienna's sister before. Ever since he dropped Sienna off last night, his mind bounced between her, her sister and worries over what the hell was going on at that cabin.

It had been close to a year ago, and he couldn't say much about the sister, didn't even know her name, but it's hard to forget a young, pretty girl bawling her eyes out in the dark.

And now that he's thought about it, the sister isn't the only one he remembers. Colby, the one who was late and helped load Jackson into the car. Troy remembers him, too. They'd rented from him before, under a different name. A business account, if he remembers correctly. That's why he hadn't picked up on it at first. If he had, he wouldn't have rented the house to them.

This was the same group that trashed Sunset Memories last year. What was supposed to be a weekend work retreat had turned into something else: a rowdy party, complete with drugs, alcohol and over two thousand dollars' worth of damage to his property. There had only been six names on the lease, but there'd been a lot more than that show up. It was after that weekend he'd started meeting his renters in person, so he could get a feel for them himself.

Not that this new practice has worked. Troy had a bad feeling about this group, but he's allowed them to rent anyway, and now he can't stop thinking about Sienna and what sort of trouble she might be in with that bunch of hooligans.

"Figured out what you want yet?" Rosie asks when she comes back to the table.

"Early Riser's Special."

"Can't beat a classic," she says, tucking his menu underneath her arm. "Just like your father."

Troy smiles. He can never decide whether he is grateful or irritated when people bring up his father. There is always a brief moment of happiness when he is reminded his father had a meaningful impact on those around him, but that is quickly followed by sadness he is no longer around.

Troy sips his soda through a straw and looks out the window. The sign for Rosie's Diner glows in neon green to attract diners from the highway, competing with the morning sun.

Inevitably, he thinks again of Sienna and her dead sister and that night from almost a year ago.

He'd been dozing in front of his television after watching *Wheel of Fortune* when he heard banging against his screen door.

"Troy? You in there?"

He jerked awake, hurrying to the door, surprised Twister and Jennings hadn't woken him before the knock did.

Gerald Buck was standing on his front porch. He owned a couple of cabins to the west, and the two often swapped odd jobs and references when the other needed help.

"Sunset Memories off Sewanee Drive. That's still your place, right?"

"Yep."

"I was driving by, and there's one hell of a party going on. I could hear the music before I even saw the place, and when I rolled down the window, the whole place smelled like bud."

"Oh, hell," Troy said, already envisioning the long night before him.

"Wanted to give you a heads-up," Gerald said. "I'm still paying off debts that after-prom party cost me last spring."

"I'll ride up that way," Troy said. "Thanks for letting me know."

Troy was half-tempted to call the police and let them deal with it, but that could cause more harm for him in the long run. If there were illegal drugs that led to arrests, or God forbid, a crime was committed, Troy would be liable for damages. It was better for him to shut it down himself.

So, he made the short drive up the mountain and was irritated when he found so many cars in the parking lot, he had to leave his own truck on the gravel road.

He stomped through the darkness and banged on the front door. Gerald was right; the place was blaring music and reeked of weed. He'd never treat his own place like this, let alone someone else's. That was the problem with his generation. No one appreciated anyone else's space. He was beginning to work himself up to the point he thought he might punch someone, then he heard a sound.

Someone was crying. He stepped off the porch, following the sounds to the side of the house. That's where he saw her. She was thin and short with dark hair pulled away from her face. Even in the darkness, he could see the leaking racoon eyes above her cheeks. Knowing what he knows now, the girl looked exactly like Sienna, although back then, she was a stranger.

"Miss, are you okay?"

She jumped back, hitting her shoulder on the side of the

house. Her hands were raised, like she was afraid Troy might attack her.

"I'm not going to hurt you," he said, raising his own hands in a surrender. "I heard you crying and wanted to make sure you aren't hurt."

"Who are you?" she called.

"Troy. I'm the owner. I'm getting complaints from other people in the area. Your group is being too loud."

The woman slapped her hand to her forehead. "Right, of course. I'm sorry. Things got a little out of hand. My company is supposed to be hosting potential investors, and it's turned into a bigger party than we expected."

Her voice was professional and kind, but there was a wavering sadness beneath it. And try as he might, Troy couldn't ignore the smeared makeup on her face. Something was terribly wrong.

"I'm more worried about you at the moment," he said. "Are you okay?"

"It's nothing." Her voice stalled with uncertainty. "I got into an argument with my friends."

Just then, the front door opened and slammed shut. There was a flurry of footsteps on the deck.

"Sammie? Are you out here?"

"Over here," she shouted, but she still sounded afraid. When two men rounded the corner, she looked even more scared.

"Who the hell are you?" one of the men asked Troy. It was too dark to make out a face.

"I'm the owner. I thought you'd prefer a visit from me over the police."

"Sorry, we'll keep it down."

"I'm getting complaints—"

"I told you we'll keep it down. Some of our guests are getting out of hand, but we're about to call it a night. Promise."

The second man remained quiet, but he was facing forward, looking past Troy, at the cowering girl behind him.

"Are you sure you're okay?" Troy asked the girl.

"Fine," she said, unconvincingly. "Like he said, we're going to call it a night."

She brushed past him and climbed the porch steps. He watched, a sinking sadness taking over him.

"We good?" the man in the dark asked.

Troy was hesitant to answer. He was still mad about the party, and part of him wanted to investigate what damage had already been done. An even bigger part of him wanted to check on the crying girl who kept insisting she was okay.

"Look, we'll be sure to pay for any damages," the guy said. "Just no cops, okay?"

Troy nodded, taking another look at the cabin before walking back to his truck. He had a bad feeling, but it was probably just his aggravation with himself for choosing such bad apples as his renters.

As promised, upon checkout, the renter left a blank check to cover any damages. It wasn't much. A few stained sheets and carpets, and he had to fumigate the place to rid it of the smoke smell. He didn't think much about that group or that night, but now that he'd met Sienna, and figured out that the crying girl was her twin sister, he couldn't stop replaying the events in his head.

What exactly had upset that girl—Samantha was her name —so much? From the looks of her, she was attractive. She ran a successful business with enough profit to rent his most luxurious cabin for a corporate retreat. And yet, she was alone in the woods, crying. She'd said she'd been in a fight with her friends, but was that true? And if it was, was it the same group of people Sienna was with this very moment?

"Hope you're hungry," Rosie says, placing the plate on his

table. The smell of the seasoned meat makes Troy's stomach roll in delight.

"Looks great, as always," Troy says, untucking the paper napkin from around his silverware and putting it in his lap.

Troy digs into his platter—bacon and eggs and hash browns and toast—but the taste is now less satisfying than he imagined.

THIRTY-SEVEN

SIENNA

Last night's sleep wasn't as restful, and when I did wake up, there were a brief, painful few moments where I forgot everything.

I forgot my sister was dead, remembering instead the former years, when I went through life with a partner at my side. I forgot I was at this cabin, far removed from my childhood home where I'm accustomed to waking up. I forgot what I came here to do.

In one brutal second, it all came rushing back. The journal and Jackson's fall and the heated exchange from yesterday. The fact my sister is gone forever, will never be with me again.

Finally, I muster the strength to get out of bed and greet the others, but the cabin is empty. Maybe they went on a walk. Wasn't that supposed to be the point of this vacation? To relax and reminisce? Take advantage of the life we have in honor of Samantha's being cut short?

Outside, there's still no one in sight. I walk around the length of the deck, seeing if I can spy where the rest of the group has gone. Hell, maybe they're just happy to be rid of me, this busybody who has ruined their trip.

I reach into my back pocket and pull out the metal screw. I'm not very knowledgeable when it comes to home improvement, but I know multiple planks wouldn't loosen on their own, and Troy confirmed on the ride back that he'd checked the balcony before we arrived. Jackson is the one always going outside for a smoke, and he's the only one I've seen all weekend leaning against the railing. Is it possible someone intended to hurt him? I can't think of any other reason why the planks would have been loosened.

If someone wanted Jackson to fall, to get hurt or possibly die, it means there must be some truth to my original suspicions. Someone has something to hide about Samantha's death. Maybe this is the real reason everyone decided to stay last night. They couldn't leave if I was still accusing them of harming her, and getting rid of Jackson meant one less person for them to fight.

I replay where everyone was when he fell. Nessa, of course, was outside with him when it happened. Could she have pushed him? I think back further, to when we were all out there before I confronted them with the diary. Jackson was the first one to join me inside. Which means any of them could have messed with the planks without me seeing. Would one of the others have seen? Are they all in on this together?

Suddenly, I remember. The journal. I'd been sitting in this very chair, the diary resting on my lap, when Jackson fell. I stand, stuffing my hands into the cushions of the seat, feeling for it. I get on my hands and knees, looking to see if it fell on the floor when I rushed outside, but there is nothing. The journal is gone, and I was so busy rushing to Jackson's defense, I didn't stop to think about it until this very moment.

I run down the hallway to my bedroom. I don't remember stopping here between Jackson's fall and riding with Troy to the hospital, but I have to check. The journal was the only evidence I had against any of them. Without it, even the screw looks weak. I lift the mattress, but there's nothing. I search the rest of the room, in case one of the others found it and put it inside my room while I was gone, but of course they wouldn't have done that.

Hopeless, I plop down onto the mattress. My eyes drift over to the framed photograph of Samantha and me.

"I'm so sorry," I say to no one.

Because the one thing Samantha did before her death was leave me her journal, and now one of her friends has taken it away.

THIRTY-EIGHT

My hand freezes on the handle of the front door.

I think I heard something, or someone, walking along the back deck. Maybe I was wrong. One of them could have stayed behind. A minute later, I see a duo of birds move from the balcony railing to the sliding glass door, their wings fluttering. They prance around for another few seconds before flying off, disappearing around the corner of the house.

I exhale in relief, my paranoia making me feel foolish.

I don't plan on hiking far. If I were to get lost in these woods, I'm not sure I'd ever find my way out. All I need is to get far enough away from the cabin to find a better phone signal. Every time I've checked my screen, I've had no bars, but I remember finding patches on my drive back with Troy. Maybe if I reach a slightly higher elevation, I'll have enough service to make a call.

After the clearing in front of the house, it's back to narrow gravel roads. I've not gone past where I currently stand, not even sure if another cabin exists higher up on the mountain, but I walk in that direction anyway, holding my phone in front of me like a compass. My sneakers crunch against the gravel. Every few steps, a pellet will slide, throwing my balance off.

I curse. Once this weekend is over, I vow to never step foot in these woods again.

After five minutes of walking, I see two bars appear on my phone. I keep holding it above my head, hoping it's not a fluke. When the bars remain, I take a seat in front of a large tree and lean against its trunk.

The receptionist at Smoky Mountain Memorial answers, and I ask to be transferred to Jackson's room. For all I know, he could still be sedated, but he's the only person I know to call. The only person I can tell about the journal and the screw without feeling like a crazy person.

When the call connects, and I hear Jackson's voice, I'm so happy I could cry.

"Thank God you're awake," I say into the phone.

"Barely." He sounds groggy but alert. "The drugs they're pumping me with are a lot stronger than the ones I planned on taking this week."

"You have a broken leg," I say. "For once, you actually need the drugs."

"So, what happened?"

I sigh in frustration. "I was hoping you could tell me."

"I remember leaning against the balcony and then feeling more pain than I've ever felt in my life," he says. "I take it I fell."

"Yes, you did. Colby and I helped you up the embankment."

"I remember parts of that, too. Thanks, even though it hurt like a bitch."

"You don't remember anything else?" I try again. "You were outside with Nessa."

"What are you getting at? Are you asking if Nessa pushed me?"

It would certainly be a lot easier to prove all this if she had. "I don't know what to think."

"No, she didn't push me. She was standing away from the railing, as I remember it."

"Well, I still think someone was trying to hurt you on purpose," I say, lowering my head. "When I got back to the cabin, I inspected the railing and saw that some of the planks were intentionally loosened."

"Really."

"Yes. And we already know everyone in the group was mad at you. And me."

"But anyone could have leaned against that railing. What makes you think they were wanting me to be the one to fall?"

"Yesterday, someone was standing outside my bedroom door listening to us. And you're the person who spent the most time on the back porch."

"Okay." He doesn't sound wholly convinced.

"And now something else is missing. Samantha's journal."

"Oh shit."

"When I got back to the house, they'd prepared some big speech about how we need to move on, grieve Samantha together. No one mentioned taking the journal."

"Which just so happens to house all their deep, dark secrets."

"Between the missing journal and the loosened planks, I'm convinced the four of them are hiding something."

There's a long pause as Jackson considers what's just been said. "I think you need to get out of there."

"What? I can't just leave."

"You have your car, don't you?"

"Yes, but—"

"Listen to what you're saying. You came here thinking one of them might have something to do with your sister's death.

Now you're accusing them of stealing Sammie's journal and trying to kill me. It isn't safe."

"This is the closest I've come to—"

There's a sound in the distance. Breaking branches and twigs, like someone or something is coming nearer.

"Sienna, what is it?"

"Hold on."

I pull the phone away from my ear and stand, carefully surveying my surroundings. Everything in the forest blends into each other. Trees. Branches. Leaves. I take a step forward, the sound of my own footsteps startling me even more.

Did someone follow me? The roadway is clear, but if someone followed me off the beaten path, I'd have no way of knowing. I remain still, listening. Wildlife skitters and scampers, birds bounce from one tree to the next, but I can't make out another person.

"Sienna! Are you there?" Jackson calls.

I bring the phone back to my ear. "I thought I heard someone. This place is making me paranoid."

"All the more reason for you to leave. Call that Troy guy and ask him for a ride if you don't feel safe."

"I can't do that. Not when I'm this close to getting answers."

"Look, if one of them is up to something, it's bound to come out. Hell, I work with all of them. We can pick another time and place for a confrontation. You on the side of a mountain with a bunch of people you can't trust isn't it."

"They've taken the diary. Without it, I have nothing. I'm going to need one of them to tell me the truth."

"Please listen to me," he says. "I'm the one who invited you up there. If something bad were to happen, I wouldn't be able to forgive myself."

"I can take care of myself," I say, slightly unsure if that's true.

"Be careful," he says before ending the call.

A feeling of hopelessness takes over when I realize I'm about to walk away from my lone connection to the outside world. I won't be able to get a strong signal back at the cabin, and I can't very well use the landline to call for help when there are so many eyes on me.

I stumble away from the treeline and back onto the gravel road. I take in my last few moments of natural beauty before going back to the group.

THIRTY-NINE

My anger builds as I march the short distance back to the cabin.

I consider Jackson's suggestion that I leave, but I know walking away without answers will only mean one thing: I'll never get them. If one of them was involved in Samantha's death, now that they know about my suspicions, they'll make sure to be around me as little as possible, and without a confession, I have no proof.

I push open the front door, the lights in the adjoining living room and kitchen dimmed. The group is sitting around the dinner table. One of Nessa's salads is in a large bowl at the center, and an opened bottle of wine stands where my place setting should be.

"There you are," Colby says. "Hope you don't mind we started lunch without you."

"Where have you been?" I look at each one of them, studying their reactions.

"We went on a hike," Nessa says.

"We thought you were sleeping," Matilda adds. "We didn't want to wake you."

They're still pretending, just as they did last night, that our issues have been resolved, but that was before I found the screw, before I realized that my sister's diary had been stolen.

"Where is it?" I ask, my voice low and mean.

Matilda, who was raising her wine glass to take a sip, pauses her hand mid-air.

"Where is what?"

"Samantha's journal. It's gone."

The four of them look at each other before turning back to me. They look genuinely confused.

"Don't you have it?" Harper asks.

"It was in the living room when Jackson fell," I say, nodding in the direction of the armchair. "I left it there, and when I went to find it this morning, it was gone."

"Are you sure you didn't misplace it?" Nessa asks. "Maybe it's in your room."

"Can we cut the bullshit!" I shout, my voice echoing inside the wooden shell of the house. "It didn't just disappear. You were the only four here. One of you has it."

"I can assure you I don't have Sammie's journal," Colby says, taking a sip of his wine without hesitation. I can see from his cold, smug demeanor, he's lying.

"Either one of you took it, or all of you did," I say.

"Why would we even want it?" Harper asks. "The only person that was obsessed with it was you."

"You'd want it because she'd written down all your secrets."

"Well, they are not secrets anymore, are they?" Nessa says, her tone sharp. "You already told us everything she had written about us. Why would we care about having it now?"

"Because if one of you hurt her, that diary is a motive. You had to keep Samantha quiet, and you stole the diary to silence me."

"*If we hurt her*," Matilda mocks. "This again. We already told you none of us did anything to Sammie."

"Well, I don't believe you," I say, reaching into my back pocket and taking the screw. "Especially after finding this."

"What's that?" Nessa asks.

"The planks outside were intentionally loosened. One of you wanted Jackson to fall."

Matilda scoffs. "Why would we want that?"

"Jackson is our friend," Harper adds. "Just like Sammie was."

"Jackson believed one of you was hiding something. He was talking to me about it in my room, just before he fell."

"You were in the living room accusing us right before he fell," Colby corrects me.

"Before that. Someone was standing outside my door listening to our conversation. They figured out Jackson was getting suspicious. Then, they loosened the planks, knowing it was only a matter of time before he'd go outside to smoke. You wanted him to fall!"

Each member of the group looks around the table again, their eyebrows raised and their jaws still.

"Sienna, do you realize how many dominos would have to fall into place for it to happen like that?" Colby asks. "Any of us could have leaned against that railing. It could have been any of us that was hurt."

But it wasn't just anyone. It was Jackson, the one person on my side. And if I believe one of them hurt my sister, then I believe they could have hurt Jackson just as easily to get him out of the way.

"You waited until I left with Jackson to take the diary," I said. "One of you is messing with me."

"Maybe you're the one who messed with the railing. You needed something dramatic to happen to prove your point. You're desperate for something to go wrong."

"Oh, fuck off. Who wouldn't be paranoid around the likes of you? All you do is lie and cheat your way to the top. You're not good friends to each other, let alone to my sister. But I'm not making this up. I know one of you hurt Jackson, and I believe one of you is involved in Samantha's death, too."

"I think Colby is onto something," Nessa says, bitterly. "Maybe you did hurt Jackson."

"Why would I want to do that?"

"There's more to your relationship than you've let on," she says. "I saw you two kissing on the balcony the first night we were here."

I'd been so stunned by his sudden advances, I'd almost forgotten Nessa saw us. The other three look at me with raised eyebrows.

"That does seem a little fishy," Harper says. "I mean, hooking up with someone you know is in love with your sister."

"We are not hooking up, okay? There is nothing going on with Jackson other than he agrees with me that the rest of you are hiding something."

"We are good friends," Nessa says. "We always have each other's backs."

"Then it *is* all of you? Tell me, what happened to my sister before she died? Why were pages ripped out of her diary? You owe me the truth!"

"Maybe you should take a seat," Matilda says, walking over to me. She reaches her hand out to touch mine, but I slap it away. In the process, her wine glass is knocked out of her hand and it shatters into a dozen pieces on the floor. "Oh no!"

"Sienna, that's enough," Colby shouts, taking a stand between me and his girlfriend. "I can't listen to this anymore. All you've done is throw accusations around like they're evidence, but they're not. You're accusing all of us of something we didn't do, and you sound crazy."

"I'm not crazy," I say, defiantly. "My sister died and I'm trying to find justice for her."

"It was an accident! There isn't any justice to find!"

"If one of you is lying—"

"No one is lying except you!" he shouts at me. "Why do you keep pretending that you're the only person that got along with Sammie? Your relationship with her was just as complicated. Maybe even more so."

"That... that isn't true."

"Isn't it?" He pauses, studying my face for a reaction. "Because I dated her for eight years. I think I'd know how she felt about her own sister. The good and the bad."

I turn from him. I turn from all of them, my mind suddenly recalling the passage of Samantha's diary I most wanted to forget.

FORTY

SAMANTHA'S DIARY

June 2022

Sometimes being a twin sucks.

People think it's really cool. They ask if we have a secret language (no), or if we can sense when the other is in trouble (no), or if we can tell what the other is thinking just by looking at them (yes).

Most days, it's insightful having a mirror image, a reflection of what your life is or could be. But when you don't like the image staring back at you, it gets tough.

I asked Sienna to join the company today. Her photography skills would be ideal for our clients, especially the ones that are shy about making their own content. Sienna could take amazing photos, and Sunshine Aesthetics would add them to the portfolio. An in-house photographer would be golden, and I can't think of anyone better to do it.

She turned me down.

She said she can't commit to something so serious. I reminded her that I'm her sister, the head of the company. If anything, I'd be providing creative freedom and financial stability all at once, but she refused.

She started rambling about some trip overseas she was planning. Said it was an opportunity to build her travel portfolio. Since when did she become a travel photographer? Why doesn't she just call it like it is and admit she's looking for a way to continue stalling?

She prides herself so much on being different and unique that she shoots down any attempt to improve her life.

And it's not like she's never traveled. She's been to Europe. Twice. She spent a summer in South America. Last winter in Canada. Funny, she didn't build her travel portfolio then.

I mean, we're pushing thirty. When is she going to grow up?

I think what hurts the most is when I even floated the idea of joining the company to my other friends—Nessa and Colby, Harper and Matilda, even Jackson—they all jumped at the opportunity. Said it was a dream to be in business with one of their best friends.

But when I ask Sienna, the person I care about most in this world, she just laughs it off.

You know, it's not easy throwing everything you have into something, building it from the ground up. It takes a lot of boring, hard work. It would be a hell of a lot easier to fly to a different continent on a whim, but we can't all be as selfish and irresponsible as my dear sister.

Sometimes I wish she'd give me more credit for what I've accomplished. I've always been willing to do that for her.

I'm angry. She has no idea how angry. When I left I swore to myself never to bring it up again, but she doesn't fully appreciate how much her rejection hurt me.

Whatever she's looking for out there, I hope she finds it. Sometimes I wish she'd just look at what's already around her—at the people already around her—and not take it for granted.

FORTY-ONE

SIENNA

"Sienna?"

Colby's voice sounds far away, even though he's only a few feet in front of me.

"You don't know what you're talking about," I say. "We had a good relationship."

"But it wasn't perfect," he says, spitefully. "Just like the rest of us. You've been pointing out our flaws all day, as though we're the enemy, but you had your issues with her, too."

I look past him, at the three women crowding around the table. They all look shocked, as though they were the ones who were just insulted, but I don't sense they feel outrage for me, rather they're impressed Colby had the nerve to put me in my place.

"We had our issues, but I still cared more about her than any of you did," I say.

"Oh yeah. Right. That's what this whole weekend is about. Showing how much *Sienna* cares."

I refuse to look at him as I stomp past. I can't listen to his insults anymore.

"Sienna, please listen," Harper says, her voice softened. She reaches out a hand, but I dodge it.

I race down the narrow corridor leading to my bedroom and slam the door shut behind me.

My heart beats hard inside my chest, my palms begin to sweat. Heat climbs the back of my neck, encircling my head.

Colby, of all people, doesn't need to lecture me about my relationship with my own sister. Even though he was her boyfriend, he was nothing more than a chain around her neck, weighing her down. I can only imagine how light and easy her life might have been had she left him long ago. She gave him the best years of her life—the last years of her life—and he wasn't even faithful to her.

And yet, he wasn't completely wrong either.

Samantha always championed my free spirit, applauded my individuality. What the rest of the world deemed weird or awkward she considered bravery. From the time we were little girls, and her golden child syndrome became known, Samantha was always the one in my corner.

And yet, despite our close bond, my actions often frustrated her. As we got older, part of her wished I'd calm down, that I could enjoy the simple, stable parts of life she'd mastered long ago. She asked me to join the company. She insisted she needed me. At the time, I thought it was her idea of charity, inviting me to join her out of pity. I didn't realize how much she wanted me to be a bigger part of her life. If I had, I wouldn't have turned her down so cruelly.

I missed the true intention behind her request, which was that she wanted more from me.

I need you. Now.

Maybe Samantha always needed me, but I was too preoccupied with myself to care.

What else did I miss? I certainly didn't know her friends caused her so much heartache. Knowing Samantha, she didn't want to let me in on the hard parts of her life, but now I wonder if she thought I couldn't handle it. If she mistook my uniqueness as weakness, and because of that, she held back the other parts of her life.

The image of my sister that's forming in my mind now is not one I want to consider. Maybe I was wrong, and she does have a closer friendship with the people here than I want to admit. At least with them, she didn't fear rejection. With them, she could be whatever version of herself she wanted to be.

This maelstrom of emotions is too much. It feels like something deep inside my chest is bound to burst, but at the same time this room is too stifling. This cabin. This place. I can barely breathe. I need to get out of here, away from these people and these thoughts. Storming to the bedroom door, I pull on the handle.

There's no give.

I freeze as momentary confusion numbs my thoughts. Again, I twist the handle, but it barely moves in either direction, the door remaining firmly shut.

Is the lock jammed? Did I slam the door so hard it's stuck? After a few more seconds of useless jangling, I call out.

"Guys? Can you hear me?" They all must be in the living room still. I can't have been in my room for more than a couple of minutes. "There's something wrong with the door."

Silence, and then Colby says, "I'm sorry, Sienna."

Sorry? What does he mean he's sorry?

"Colby?" I begin banging again, my mind racing with possibilities. Did he close it by mistake? I knew there was a lock from the inside, but I never realized it locked from the outside, too. Surely, the others can hear the desperation in my voice. The fear. "Colby! Open the door."

"This is all your fault, you know." I can tell from the tone of his voice the locked door is the farthest thing from his mind, and that inconvenience doesn't stop him from spewing his vitriol. "If you hadn't brought that diary, none of this would have happened. You're stirring up drama that's long buried."

"It's not long buried to me," I say, plainly. Is he still focusing on the diary right now? Even when he knows I'm locked inside my bedroom? "I was trying to do what's best for my sister."

"And you think making everyone upset is what's best?"

"I'm only trying—"

"You're tearing our lives apart, and for what? Because of a few bitchy words your sister wrote about us. Talking about her shitty friends and her crush on Jackson. Calling me *a mediocre* lover. Is it really worth ruining our lives?"

I inhale deeply, trying not to let my anger get the best of me. It slowly sinks in what's happening. This isn't a mistake. Colby deliberately locked me in here. My fists bang harder against the door. "Colby! Let me out."

"You don't have to stay in there long," he says. "Just until you come to your senses."

"My senses? Colby, let me out of this fucking room. Right now!"

My breathing gets faster. My chest feels like it's expanding, all while the walls around me are closing in. I clear my throat.

"Harper? Nessa?" I call out, knowing at least one of them must still be standing around, listening as Colby holds me prisoner. Weakly, I say, "Matilda?"

"I think we all need some space," one of them says, but I can't decipher which one. The voice is small, weak. Unwilling.

"We're not doing anything to you, Sienna," Colby says, his voice stronger, in control. "Maybe some time alone will calm you down, and then we can have a productive conversation."

My eyes bounce around the room, pinging from one wall to the next. Already, it feels like the narrow space is closing in on me, stealing my breath, my agency, my sanity. I can't bear to be in here another second.

"Colby, please." I struggle to make my voice neutral, rational. "Don't leave me in here."

"We'll be back," he says. "Soon."

His footsteps move away from the door, an innocuous sound in a normal situation, but loud as sirens under these circumstances. I keep listening until the sound is faint, nothing.

I'm all alone.

FORTY-TWO

They've left.

It's the same silence I remember from this morning, but more dangerous now. I feel my pockets, an immediate reaction to find my phone, but it isn't here. I'd stormed into this room so quickly, I must have left it in the living room. Even if I did have it, reception is sparse. I had to hike more than ten minutes to get a hold of Jackson.

I keep shouting, hoping Colby will have a shred of remorse, or hoping someone else will hear me and let me out. But there is no one else. Even if Nessa and Harper and Matilda hear my screams, would they release me? Or did they know what Colby planned on doing? They could all be in this together.

I listen, trying to decide if anyone is around. There's nothing but quiet. Even the loud forest has been blocked by the walls.

It settles in how alone I am. The only people that know I'm here may not have any intention of letting me out. And what is Colby's purpose, exactly? What does he plan on doing with me? I think back to everything he said, before I realized I'd been tricked and panic set in. He said he wanted me to come to my senses, but what does that mean?

Then I remember something else Colby said about what was written in Samantha's diary. He mockingly referred to himself as a mediocre lover and talked about her crush on Jackson—those were two details from the diary I never shared.

I think back to the tone in his voice when he mentioned those details, his wounded ego on full display. Those words bothered him because they came directly from Samantha, and there's only one way he would have known about them: if he read the diary himself.

My beliefs have wavered this weekend, like a candle trying to keep light in the wind, but those comments prove Colby read her diary, and the only time he would have had to do that was after it went missing. If he took her diary, or if they all did, it proves they're still hiding something. If I ever want to know what that is, I have to get out of this room.

There's only one other escape route; the small balcony across from my bed. I sling open the door and begin screaming, hoping someone nearby might hear me. It's wasted breath. The cabin is too secluded for anyone else to hear my cries. We've not passed another camper, hiker, renter since we arrived here. It's only the six of us—five of us now—alone in these woods.

I move onto my second option, which is to somehow make it from the small balcony to the ground below. It's a far drop, perhaps even farther than the tumble Jackson took yesterday. Still, it's my only option. If I can get my legs around the railing, I could lower myself down, slowly. From that point, it would be only a small drop. I might hurt something, but it wouldn't be deadly, and then I'd be free.

I swing one leg over the side, straddling the railing like it's a saddle. This isn't my first time descending the side of a house. I did it plenty of times during my teenage years, sneaking out that large window in Samantha's room. I take a deep breath, trying to find my balance before I bring my leg to the other side.

I can't. Fear, solid and slow, keeps me in place. My body feels like it's teetering, even though there's little to no wind. I think about Jackson, the painful moaning sounds he made as we carried him over the hill.

I think of Samantha, of what we were told about her death. When she fell, her death wasn't instant. She remained there for hours. Bleeding, dying. In pain and alone. I look down, at the green grass below, the wispy hammock between the trees. If I make a wrong step and fall, can I trust the others to help me? Or would they leave me to die, wounded and broken, as I believe one of them did to Samantha.

That horrible image I've conjured of Samantha every night since her death returns. I'm so very close to suffering the same fate as her. A wave of anxiety rushes through me, and before I can stop myself, I swing my dangling leg back, until my body is placed firmly on the balcony. I hurry inside the bedroom, my prison, it seems, fall to my knees, and cry.

My throat is raw from all the screaming.

There's no way to tell time, but hours must have passed. The bright bursts of sunlight streaming in through the balcony door have become weaker. Now there's a musky glow, and I fear soon I'll be seeing streaks of moonlight.

I can't believe they've locked me in here, especially for this long. All this time, I've not heard them. I wonder if they've left the mountain completely, if they'll ring Troy or someone else to let me out, put as much distance as possible between themselves and me, so by the time I do get out, whatever allegations I bring against them will be deemed irrational.

Maybe they don't plan on telling anyone about me at all.

I should never have come here. In all the emotional, lonely hours I've spent in this room, that's the one certainty I return to. My presence has caused nothing but more problems, and hasn't brought me any closer to finding justice for my sister. What happened to her remains a mystery, and even though I'm more convinced than ever her friends are at fault for something, I'll never be able to prove it. Even the diary is gone.

The photograph of the two of us sits on my nightstand. Two faces, so similar, and yet the souls behind them so different. Even on the day this was taken, she didn't want to be photographed, but I insisted. How many times did I ignore the boundary between us, putting my own selfish needs and wants before hers? Even now, my one-sided, desperate need to find out what happened to her has caused more problems than it's solved. Maybe all this paranoia and suspicion stems from the fact I can't accept my sister is gone, and that I wasn't there for her when she needed me most.

Without thinking, I scoop up the frame and hurl it across the room.

It hits one of the panels square on, chipping the wood before crashing to the floor, the glass plate splintering into pieces.

Then I sit on my bed, head in my hands, and cry.

I walk over to the wall and begin to pick up the pieces. The photograph isn't damaged, but the frame is ruined. I lift up the broken pieces, careful not to cut my skin with the shattered glass. The left side of the frame hangs to the side before breaking off and falling to the floor. That's when I see something poking out of the cardboard backing behind the picture.

I turn over the broken frame in my hand, taking a closer look. Something is balled up and tucked tight between the frame and the picture. I slip my fingers into the small area and pull out three wadded up sheets of notebook paper.

Unfolding them, my heart does somersaults in my chest as I recognize the handwriting.

It's Samantha's.

These are the final, missing pages of her journal.

FORTY-THREE

SAMANTHA'S LETTER

October 2022

Dear Sienna,

I've debated whether to write this. You're supposed to be having the time of your life right now, and the last thing I want is for you to be worried about me, but you're also the only person I can trust.

I don't want a constant reminder of what happened, and yet, even if I tried, I don't think I could ever forget. The whole, horrible event keeps playing in my mind. Again, and again and again.

It was a last-minute trip, planned by Colby. After weeks of trying, he'd managed to woo his dream investor, Roy Balding. To seal the deal, he wanted to impress Balding and his team with one of our famous getaways. All we could find last-minute was a cabin in the woods a few hours away—a place called Sunset Memories.

The trip was so thrown together, not even the entire team could come. That's fine. It was supposed to be nothing more than a few fancy meals and drinks and business talks. But that first night, everything took a turn. Balding had brought a whole team of people with him, which was never part of the plan. He might have been the wealthiest investor we'd ever courted, but there was a dangerous vibe around him I didn't trust. Colby and the girls were busy chatting with the friends he'd brought, and Colby insisted I be the one to handle Balding.

"You're the leader. He wants to hear from you," he said. "I know you have what it takes to impress him."

But I wasn't on my game. There'd been too much drinking earlier in the night. There had been drugs, too, even though I didn't partake. Everyone was so wasted and beginning to blare loud music, hanging around the balcony outside.

Balding and I decided to go to the basement where it was quieter. I needed to talk business; about all the ways his investment could take Sunshine Aesthetics to the next level.

But once we were alone, there was no talking.

I can't bear to go into everything that happened. Those are the minutes I keep replaying in my mind, but he forced me to do things I didn't want to do. I begged. I cried. I screamed. My closest friends were only a few feet away, and yet, because of the loud music and partying, they couldn't hear.

When it was over, Balding smiled. "Who says you can't mix business with pleasure, right?"

I ran to the bathroom and threw up. I wanted to hop in the bath, soak until I felt clean. Instead, I marched up the stairs, looking for my friends. I had every intention of telling them what happened, but when I reached them, none of them would listen to me. I ended up outside by myself, crying. I didn't go back inside until the cabin owner showed up and chastised us for being too loud. If only he knew what other crimes had been committed that night.

I felt foolish. This was the type of thing that happened to

younger girls. It didn't happen to women pushing thirty, to women who ran their own business, women who had a boyfriend in the next room. Of course, what happened to me shouldn't happen to any woman, regardless of the circumstances.

Later that night, when I told Colby, he acted shocked, angered. Deep down, I wonder if he didn't suspect what happened. After all, Balding and him came looking for me outside. He saw me crying. He must have known something was wrong.

The next morning, I told the girls what happened. I expected my friends to rally around me. Instead, they told me to keep quiet. They ran through a long list of potential problems going up against Balding could bring. Most importantly, it could hurt our business.

It's been three days. Three horrible days and nights of replaying what happened, debating what I should do next. As I write this, I'm in my childhood bedroom. I keep thinking about the little girl who spent her childhood here. I know now I was always prone to peer pressure, so concerned about what my peers thought about me.

But you, Sienna, were never like that, and if you were here with me right now, like I wish you were, you would never allow me to act like a victim. You'd push me to go forward, no matter what the impact on my business and friendships, and do the right thing. You would be outraged enough for the both of us. You'd tell me what I need to do and never once make me feel like I'm weak for doing it. I came home to see Dad and Ma, but I don't think I can bear to tell either of them what happened.

Not yet.

I have to go to the police first. I'm driving back to the condo tonight, and I plan on going to report Roy Balding for his crimes tomorrow. I can only imagine how outraged you'll be when you read this, but know by the time this letter reaches you, the hard part will be over. I'll have gone to the police, and I hope that's enough to make you proud. We'll figure out the next steps together, once you're home.

Now, I'm going to drive home. The world will look different tomorrow, but maybe it's time for a change.

FORTY-FOUR

SIENNA

Tears stream down my face as I try to make sense of what I've just read. There's a burning anger inside of me, directed at no one and everyone all at once. I've never felt so helpless; I can only imagine how my sister felt.

Samantha was assaulted. She didn't deserve it—no woman does. The horror is made worse by the fact my sister always carried herself with caution, care. On the night it happened, she was surrounded by people she trusted. She should have been safe, but she wasn't, and then when she went to those same people for support, they refused. After everything they'd been through together—years of friendship, trials and triumphs, vacations and the business—they abandoned her.

I was the only person Samantha could count on, which is why she wrote this letter. She wanted me to know what happened to her.

I need you. Now.

But she never ended up sending it. Why not? And why was it hidden inside a framed photograph? Her plan had been to return to her condo and go to the police the next day. Something, or someone, must have stopped her. Perhaps she had an unexpected visitor at the condo that night. Maybe she knew she was in danger, or at least that she was vulnerable, so she hid the letter in a place where only I would find it, much like she left the diary in the broken bench at our parents' house. That's the only plausible scenario for why she would have hidden it.

Someone stopped her from mailing the letter.

Someone stopped her from going to the police.

And now I'm locked inside this bedroom, at the mercy of the very people who I know abandoned my sister in her time of need. Earlier this weekend, as I rattled off each of their individual secrets in the diary, the group remained silent. Waiting. This was the secret they feared I'd reveal, because they know it's an act I'll never be able to forgive. This entire weekend, I've been played. Even when I believed I had the upper hand, it was this catastrophic event they had to keep me from uncovering.

There is no legal punishment for not helping your friend in the aftermath of a tragedy, but that situation highlights just how morally bankrupt each one of them are. Coming forward about Samantha's rape could have repercussions for the company, too. Not only did it happen on a company-sponsored trip, but the new majority stakeholder for Sunshine Aesthetics is her rapist.

Exhausted, I sit on the floor, pulling my knees to my chest. I lower my head and try to breathe deeply. Nothing about this weekend unfolded the way I thought it would. I'm no closer to understanding the truth about how Samantha died, and what I did find out about her final days only breaks my heart more.

I feel a bundle of sobs forming in my chest, and I'm too weak to fight them down. I'm too weak to do anything but sit alone and cry. They were her closest friends and they betrayed her. What will they do to me?

I close my eyes and try to steady my thoughts. I think about Samantha, what she would do in this situation. Truthfully, she'd be the one sitting on the floor, crying into her hands. She'd be the one looking at me, asking for help. And if she were with me,

I'd have the strength to get us both out of the situation. Her fear and sadness would strengthen me, give me the courage to fight for both of us.

I realize that's the exact predicament we're in. Samantha is no longer here to fight her battles. There's only me. Even if I'm too weak to fight for myself, I'd never give up on her. That's why I have to get through this, because Samantha's legacy is at stake, just as much as my own life.

I stand, searching every corner of the room, hopeful I'll find something that can get me out of here. There's a large dresser across from my bed. I sling open the drawers, which are mostly empty, searching for something, anything. The bottom left drawer is heavier than the rest, filled with random pieces of paper and batteries and old remotes. A junk drawer of sorts. Near the bottom, I find a small Tupperware filled with random nails and screws. I pinch a few, and get down on my knees, fiddling with the lock.

It's useless, so I start again, this time looking for something bigger, an item that could break down the door. The room is so sparse, little more than a bed, dresser and rocking chair, none of which would be useful in breaking down a door. I drop to my knees, looking under the bed for something useful. A folded air mattress sits on the floor at the foot of the bed. Behind that, there's a metal box that looks like it's filled with fishing equipment, but I'm afraid it's too light to do any damage.

Then, at the very back, I see it. A metal fire extinguisher, nestled beside the foot of the headboard and the wall. I grab it, the weight of the cold metal pleasing me. I bang on the door again with a hand. The wood is hollow and weak, which means the lock is likely flimsy. With just the right amount of force, I might be able to break it open.

I hold the fire extinguisher high above my head, and bring it down hard on the brass doorknob. The material bends, but doesn't break. I'm afraid I might have broken whatever mechanism allows the knob to turn, making it even harder for me to break free. I raise the fire extinguisher again, this time holding it at an angle, so that it swings against the knob in a downward trajectory, aiming to push whatever is keeping me in, out.

The sound of the impact gives me hope. For a split second, I see the door give. I raise my arms over my head a third time, bringing down the fire extinguisher.

This time, the knob falls to the ground and the door swings open. I'm rooted to the spot, stunned that it worked. I'm free.

FORTY-FIVE

TROY

After an afternoon of running errands, Troy still isn't ready to return home. He settles for dinner and drinks at the Salty Moose Tavern.

It isn't very often he drinks in public anymore. Prices have surged since the pandemic; he can purchase a six-pack for the same price as a large draft. Really, he isn't that big a drinker. Alcohol inhibits a person's ability to work, and work is always his priority.

"That's never a good sign, is it?"

"What?"

The barmaid is staring at the television in the corner of the room, turning up the volume. Troy follows her gaze. The local news is reporting a small fire has broken out east of the mountain. The cause is undetermined, but due to increasing wind velocity since the afternoon, fire crews had been sent to stop the damage before it burned out of control. Not too much to worry about.

Yet.

When your entire life has been ruined by wildfires, your entire community shattered, a small news report is enough to bring back long-buried memories. Not only for Troy, but likely for all the local diners at the Salty Moose.

"You still have cabins up that way?" the bartender asks.

"Yep."

"Probably nothing to worry about," she says, but her voice isn't believable.

That's what they all thought last time. The fires would stop. Fire crews would put them out. No one imagined the blaze would continue, destroying homes and lives in never-before-seen fashion, at least around these parts.

The bell above the front door dings as a new customer walks inside. The barmaid walks to the other side of the bar to greet her new customer.

Between the local news reporting on wildfires in the area and his incessant thoughts of Sienna's sister a year ago, Troy needs the beer to calm his mind, mellow his senses. By the time he arrives home, maybe he'll be able to drift off to sleep without effort.

Even hearing the word *wildfire* brings back memories he wishes to suppress. Memories of his father, both good and bad. Troy was in middle school when his father bought their first rental cabin. The way he beamed with pride, you would have thought he'd purchased a vacation home for him, not other travelers. Where Troy's father grew up, it was rare for a person to buy their own home, let alone two. He felt like a king. Troy worked as his apprentice even back then, mowing the cabin's lawn in the springs and summers, even cleaning the place at times. And his father explained the business side of things, too.

That first rental cabin brought in enough money for them to purchase a second cabin, and then a third. By the time Troy had graduated and enlisted in the military, his father was able to leave his job at the plant to look after the cabins full-time.

After his final shift, the family of two celebrated with a country fried steak and sweet tea at Rosie's Diner. Troy was in

his second year of the army, on leave, and grateful to be celebrating this major milestone with his father.

"Look at your pops, the businessman," his father beamed,
sipping his tea through a straw.

Things were looking up for the first time in a long while.
His father was proud of what he'd accomplished, which was far
more than any other member of their family ever had. He'd
even promised to make Troy his official business partner, whenever his time with the military was complete.

Then the fires hit.

More than fifteen thousand acres of land was burned up
and ruined in the matter of a couple of days. It was the largest
wildfire to ever hit the area, even made the local news and led to
a celebrity-run telethon.

Troy was stationed in Germany when he heard about it in
passing.

"Country boy," one of his brothers-in-arms called to him.
"Aren't you from Tennessee?"

Like the rest of the world, he watched the coverage, feeling
useless an entire ocean away. He wasn't able to get a hold of his
father until the following day. The relief he felt at knowing his
father was alive quickly subsided.

"Everything is gone," his father said, an aching devastation
in his voice. "The fire took everything."

"The people. Are they okay?"

"Yeah. We evacuated them to the local church. None of our
renters were injured, but the cabins..." His voice trailed away.
"They're all burnt to the ground."

"Hang tight, Dad," Troy told him over the phone. "The
whole world is chipping in to help out the area. And there's
insurance—"

"It won't be enough," his father broke in. "I put all my
savings from the first two properties into purchasing the third
one. The insurance money won't be enough to cover it."

Troy knew without it being said what this meant to his father. This was far more than three buildings being leveled to ash and debris. It was his father's dream that had gone up in smoke, too.

Troy had a sinking feeling in his stomach. This was the very reason he hadn't wanted to enlist in the first place. It had always been the two of them, and now his father was going through a complete crisis on his own, and Troy was too far away to do anything about it.

"I'll be home in the next two months," he said. "Everything is going to be okay."

But as Troy got off the phone that night, he knew that wasn't true. He'd felt something awful and painful inside, something he'd never felt before.

A week later, he'd gotten the phone call.

After the rains came in to end the fires and most of the debris was cleaned up, Troy's father had driven to the very spot where his first cabin had sat. He'd put his gun in his mouth and pulled the trigger.

Troy was able to come home on bereavement leave, but there was nothing left for him there. His father, gone. The cabins, gone. Even the other places he remembered from his childhood, most of them were damaged, destroyed or going out of business due to financial burdens. Troy had traveled across the world to ensure a better future for himself, his father and his country, all while his hometown went up in smoke.

Troy struggled to understand his father's suicide for a long time. It made the last leg of his military career unbearable, knowing there was no home to return to when his time was up. He took up reading self-help books about mental health and grief. Over time, he started to understand what his father must have been feeling in those final moments. The despair and desperation. It wasn't the loss of money that had driven him to take his own life; it was the lack of purpose. His father's livelihood had been stolen, and at sixty, he didn't feel he could start over.

Still, Troy believes if he'd been in town when it happened, he would have been able to make a difference. Maybe, just maybe, he could have saved his father.

When he did return, he had the small amount of money he'd inherited after his father's death and the money he'd saved during his time overseas. He could have done anything with the money. Gone back to school. Started a business of his own. Instead, he bought his first cabin. He'd so admired watching his father build a business from the ground up, even if it had all been ripped away overnight. He wanted to prove to his father, even in death, that it was possible to rebuild.

When the news reports talked about the damage to the soil and the wildlife and the economy, they didn't understand that the fires had taken far, far more from him.

FORTY-SIX

SIENNA

The house is quiet, eerily so, as though the hours I spent crying and screaming to be let out of the room stole some of the life within the walls.

I storm through the hallway, kitchen, and living room, a madwoman on a mission. I grab my phone from the table and search the house. I must confront them all. Now.

About why they locked me in my bedroom in the first place.

About what happened to Samantha. Here. In this very cabin.

No luck. The house is empty, which explains the strange silence. Is it possible they've finally taken the opportunity to leave? Were they really going to leave me stranded in that room with no way out?

I hurry out the front door, taken aback by the approaching darkness. When I was last outside, the sun was bright, a beaming spotlight overhead. Now it's beginning to set behind the trees, the light-blue sky fading to an ominous gray.

That's when I hear it. Footsteps coming from the other side of the cars in the driveway. I march closer, and find all four of them—Colby, Matilda, Harper and Nessa—circled around the firepit, although there's no blaze at the center. They're gathered around talking, likely trying to figure out what to do next.

Nessa sees me first. She stands quickly, her eyes wide, white saucers. "Sienna. What are you doing?"

"I broke down the damn door," I cry, anger fueling every step.

Colby stands next, holding his hands out between us. An apology or a form of protection, I'm not sure. "What I did was wrong," he says, and I assume he's talking about holding me prisoner all afternoon. "I only wanted everyone to calm down."

He dares to put his hand on my forearm.

I yank it back with a raging force. My anger over being locked in the bedroom will have to wait. Right now, I'm confronting them all with the truth about Samantha.

"You've been here before."

"What?" There's a look of confusion on his face.

"You came to this exact cabin right before Samantha died."

"It... well." He stumbles over his words. "I never said this was our first time in the area."

"We take several trips every year for business," Nessa adds. "You know that."

Yes, they've skated around the idea they've been here before, even outright lied about never staying at Sunset Memories. Now that I know the truth, their peculiar behavior from earlier makes sense. Their somber reactions on that first day upon seeing the cabin. Harper gliding through the kitchen. Nessa crying in the basement.

They've all been here before. And they all know what happened to my sister during their last trip.

"You said you've never been to *this* cabin before. That's a lie. What happened the last time you were here?" I ask, keeping my voice level. "What happened on the last trip you took before my sister died?"

"Nothing," Harper says, too quickly. "Nothing happened."

I lift my hand, clutching the torn pages from my sister's journal.

"Stop. Lying. To me."

"What is that?" Matilda asks.

"The pages that were missing from Samantha's journal. I just found them."

"What?" Colby looks confused. "How?"

"She tore them out to write me a letter, but ended up hiding it in a picture frame. The same one I brought with me this weekend. She put them there because she wanted me to know." I wait, relishing the understanding, shocked looks on their faces. "I'm going to ask again. What happened that weekend?"

"What is she talking about?" Matilda asks Colby.

"You should know. You were all here," I say.

"I wasn't," Matilda says, looking at Nessa and Harper with the same confused look. "The trip was last-minute. I had my brother's wedding that weekend and couldn't make it. Jackson wasn't here either."

"Of course, he wasn't. He had another stint in rehab," Colby says, "that didn't work."

If that's true, Matilda doesn't know what happened to my sister. She doesn't know the horrible details that were written in that journal. Unless one of the others told her. Her agitated reaction makes me think they did not.

"Go ahead, Colby. Tell your new girlfriend what happened to your old girlfriend right before she died."

"Listen, I don't know what is on that piece of paper—" Harper starts, but I cut her off, tired of their excuses.

"Okay, I guess it will be me. Roy Balding. Does that name ring a bell?"

"Of course, I know Roy Balding. His company bought Sunshine Aesthetics after Samantha died," Matilda says. She's watching me in a more intense way than she ever has before.

Like me earlier this weekend, she wants answers. "What does he have to do with anything?"

"Nothing," Colby says, his voice harsh and final.

My mouth falls open, and I'm not sure if I want to scream or cry. My body aches in pain as all the pieces finally fall into place.

"How could you let him take ownership of Samantha's company after what he did to her?"

"Someone tell me what is going on!" Matilda screams.

"Roy Balding was on the trip, wasn't he? The party got a little out of hand. *Uncontrollable* was the word Samantha used. While the three of you were off schmoozing with other investors and getting lit yourselves, you left her alone with Roy. And he raped her."

"That's not what happened!" Nessa shouts.

"Samantha said that's what happened, and I believe her."

"Samantha was raped?" Matilda sits unsteadily.

"Like she said, things got out of hand," Colby says, massaging his brow. "We didn't know what had happened until the next morning."

"That's a lie!" I shout. "Samantha wrote it down for me. She told you about it that night, and you told her she was overreacting." I turn my anger from Colby to Harper and Nessa. "And she told you, too, but you convinced her to keep quiet."

"We'd all had too much to drink," Nessa said. "It's not that I didn't believe her, but we had no proof."

"She told you what happened! She told her boyfriend and her closest friends. And what did you do about it?"

"Please, tell me you reported this," Matilda says, although she must already know the answer.

"They didn't. They told her it would hurt her reputation and the rest of the business if she came forward. And that's not even the worst part," I say. "Two weeks after Samantha's death, you accepted Balding's offer. You put my sister's rapist on the board of the company she created, and then dared to call your-selves her friends."

"We were her friends," Harper says. "We handled the situa-tion the best we could, but we couldn't let one bad situation tear down the rest of the company. With Samantha gone, we needed someone else to step in."

"You could have found another investor. Samantha could have gone to the police and prosecuted Balding for what he did."

"It wasn't just about the money," Nessa says. "You know how assault allegations end up. He said, she said. There's no way Roy Balding is going to go down for rape, and all it would have done is scare away future investors. No one wants to do business with a company known for causing legal problems."

"She was attacked! Your friend of almost a decade." I look at Harper. "For you, it was even longer. You'd known her since she was a girl. That wasn't more important than the business?"

"In the moment, no," Colby says, with finality. "When Sammie told us what happened, we were horrified. Especially me. I mean, she was my girlfriend. It enraged me someone would harm her like that."

He says it with the same repulsion he might have over someone ruining another possession of his. Denting his car, soiling an heirloom tablecloth.

"If you were so enraged, why didn't you do anything about it?"

"Because Sammie had just gone through a trauma and wasn't thinking with her right mind. The real Sammie wouldn't want anything to ruin the business, even this. So we went ahead with the deal because we thought that was best."

"Sienna is right," Harper says. "We should have done more to help her."

For once this weekend, I feel seen. Like someone is finally starting to understand my desperation. But then she continues.

"None of us knew how much she was hurting. We should have taken time to be with her, make sure she was okay, but we didn't." She pauses. "And that's why she killed herself."

"What?"

"Sammie killed herself," Nessa says. "Because of what happened and because of what we did to her."

It feels like my body is burning from the inside out, radiating with anger and outrage and disbelief. Sweaty palms clench tighter around the letter.

"She wouldn't. Sammie would never—"

"*This* is the secret we've been trying to keep," Colby said. "This is what we didn't want you or anyone else to know. Sammie didn't fall over the balcony. And she wasn't pushed. She jumped, because of what happened that weekend."

"You think Sammie took her own life?"

I'm surprised the question doesn't come from me, but from Matilda. This is all new information to her, I remember. She must be experiencing the same, unpredictable waves of emotion.

"Yes," Nessa says. "I mean, none of us know. We weren't there. It could have been an accident, but knowing how upset she was about what happened with Roy—"

"We don't want to think of Sammie like that," Harper butts in. "What happened to her in the weeks before she died... the headspace she was in before her death... that wasn't the Sammie we all know and love."

"It isn't true. Samantha would have reached out to me if she was struggling."

"She tried, but you weren't here," Colby reminds me, coldly. "You were in Europe, remember? She left you that voice mail instead. She visited your parents the weekend she died. I thought at the time she was maybe talking to them about it. After she died, I thought she went there to say goodbye."

I'm quick to call him a liar again, but then I think about

what he said. She did try calling me, but we never made contact. Her visit to my parents was uncommon. And she wrote about what happened in a letter she never ended up sending.

I need you. Now.

"She'd been drinking heavily that night. Alone," Nessa says, interrupting my thoughts, adding another believable layer to the possibility. "Sammie wasn't a big drinker. Clearly, she was trying to numb the pain."

"We didn't want you to know any of this," Harper says. "We were trying to protect you."

"Protect me?" The anger begins building again. "You should have protected *her*. You discouraged her from going to the police, and then took money from the man who assaulted her."

"You're right," Nessa says, plainly. "It's a guilt we've carried for the past year."

"Samantha was raped. And all of you knew?" Matilda asks. Her voice is high-pitched, disbelieving. She almost sounds like a child, the world she thought she knew crashing around her.

"Jackson didn't know," Colby says. "The rest of us were there that night."

"And the three of you believe she killed herself because of this?"

"Yes," Harper says.

Matilda locks eyes with me, only briefly. Watery pain is building in her stare.

"She was our friend." She looks at Colby, as though seeing him for the first time. "She was your girlfriend! And you didn't listen to her."

"We messed up!" Colby cries. "None of us thought she would hurt herself. You have to believe me."

"Why would I believe you?" Matilda says coldly. "You lie about everything. About what happened to Sammie. About what happened between us."

"What?" I ask.

Matilda gives Colby a defiant final look. "We started sleeping together the summer before Sammie died. Colby kept saying they were on the verge of breaking up, that they only stayed together because of the company. It was just another lie, and I've felt like an awful friend since then, especially since Sammie died so soon after. But *my* betrayal is nothing compared to what the rest of you did to her."

The truth leaves Matilda's lips so easily now, all their tightly guarded lies unfurling.

"We were trying to think about the big picture," Harper says. "We didn't mean for any of it to happen."

"Enough. I don't want to hear any more. From any of you!"

Matilda takes off running toward the forest, disappearing into the darkening night. The others take off after her, and I start chasing after them.

FORTY-SEVEN

The darkness in the forest is like nothing I've ever seen before. Once entering the canopy of trees across from the cabin, it's like someone has pulled a tight covering over my head. I can hardly see my hands as I hold them out in front of my face.

"Matilda?" I hear Colby's voice calling, from somewhere in front of me.

"Mattie?" calls out a voice from behind, Nessa.

I hear footsteps as I presume Nessa and Harper run past me. I follow them, quickly losing sight of their silhouettes. I'm alone in these woods, and yet not alone; it only feels that way, because everyone is hidden in the night.

I walk toward the treeline, following the same path I took earlier when I called Jackson. It's amazing how different the place looks now under the cloak of night. Like an entirely different world. Every few seconds, I hear Matilda's name being called out by the others, but everyone is spread apart and it's difficult to figure out where they are. Either way, it doesn't sound like Matilda has been found.

"Mattie!" someone calls. Her name echoes through the forest in random intervals.

I run in the direction where I think the voices came from, until my body connects with something hard. It's Colby.

"Did you see where she went?" I ask.

"No. I can't see anything," he says, shaken and out of breath. "And what's that smell?"

A heavy scent is in the air all around us. I hadn't noticed it before. My eyes begin to water, and my throat constricts. "I think it's smoke. Is something burning?"

"I don't know," he says, looking from left to right. He doesn't care about our surroundings, only finding Mattie. "It's too dark for her to be out here by herself."

"She won't go far," I say, using the light on my phone as a guide. There's nothing, no one. Only the two of us, alone in the woods.

"There have to be some flashlights back at the house," he says. "We need more than our phones if we want to find her."

Before I can respond, he takes off, and I let him. We're scattered throughout the forest with the same mission: find Matilda. Still, I'm aware of the trauma I've experienced tonight at the hands of Colby, being locked inside my bedroom for several hours.

And now I know about the trauma he and the others inflicted on Samantha when she was alive. I recall passages of Samantha's letter, and every time I do, my stomach roils with sickness, my chest fills with anger. Her closest friends knew about her assault but were more concerned with covering it up than getting her justice.

Most of her friends, anyway. Matilda claims she didn't know; she didn't join them on the first trip to Sunset Memories. Based on her emotional reaction, the fact she admitted to covering her affair with Colby and then took off into the woods, I'm apt to believe her.

As I replay the confrontation in my mind, I consider Colby and Harper and Nessa's theory about what happened to her.

They believed Samantha's death was a suicide. That she was so overtaken with grief about the assault she ended her own suffering.

My first reaction is to not believe them, but part of me wonders, could it be true? I imagine the enormity of what my sister was dealing with, accept the fact she was forced to handle her emotions on her own. Her boyfriend minimized what had happened. Her friends urged her not to press charges. Her sister was halfway around the world.

She turned to alcohol, which explains why she was so intoxicated at the time of her death. The loneliness she must have felt in those final weeks... I can't even imagine. Is that why she reached out to my parents? Was she searching for some form of familiarity to help make sense of things? Or did she return home that weekend to say goodbye? Maybe the diary and the letter and everything to which I've been clinging were all ways for her to say goodbye.

But.

Why would she write me a letter, one she never got the chance to send? Why would she leave me a voice mail? If she planned on harming herself, if she knew that phone call would be the last communication between us, wouldn't she have said goodbye?

I need you. Now.

No, Samantha wasn't giving up. She was pushing forward, and she needed my help to do it. That's why she was reaching out. Someone stopped her, and no matter how Colby and Harper and Nessa try to mess with my head, I know it was one of them that did it.

Suddenly, my phone pings, startling me. I jump back but am relieved to find I have enough service for a message to come through.

A series of messages, actually. From Jackson.

Where are you?

Are you okay?

Have you been evacuated?

Evacuated? He'd wanted me to leave earlier, but that's a strange choice of words.

I hastily type out a reply:

At the cabin. Trying to get answers.

I hit send, but the message turns green, a small icon beside the words letting me know my message is waiting to be sent. The cell service left just as quickly as it came, and I curse again.

I check the time, aware it's getting later. How long have we been out here searching for Matilda in the dark? Thirty minutes? Closer to an hour?

A scream cuts through the night, loud and angry. Human. It's so frightening, I'm paralyzed from taking a step further. I turn around, facing the house, not expecting to see anything, and yet I can see the subtle outline of our cabin. A strange light, orange and raging, acts as a backdrop, like the setting sun from earlier, and yet it's evening. Far too late for that.

Jackson was right. This is getting too dangerous for me to handle on my own, and now one of the group members could very well be lost in the forest. For all we know, the others could get lost looking for her. Our sense of direction is too fragile. I race to the cabin, back to safety and light.

I rush through the open front door, calling around to see if Matilda, or anyone else, turned back around without me realizing.

No one calls out in response.

I rush to the kitchen where the landline hangs from the

wall, but when I put the receiver to my ear, I'm met with a dull tone. The line is dead.

"Shit," I say, pressing the dial button over and over.

I slam the phone against the wall and pull my cell out of my pocket. No service. Still.

"Shit," I say again. Maybe it's my adrenaline from finally accusing her fake friends, or my concern over Matilda being lost in the woods, but this situation seems to have escalated in a way I wasn't expecting. I'm frightened, wishing, too late, I'd heeded Jackson's warning.

Something captures my attention off the back porch. I venture through the sliding glass door, trying to get a better look.

What I see grips my insides with fear.

The sky is a sickly orange, the silhouette of black trees standing tall against the backdrop. Smoke billows from the ground up, like clouds that have lost their way.

The forest is on fire.

FORTY-EIGHT

TROY

It has been a long time since Troy spent an entire evening in a bar.

He hasn't been drinking the whole time, is far too old for that kind of behavior. After his second IPA, he switched to sweet tea and an order of cheese sticks. Still, he can't pull himself away from the barstool, finds too much comfort in being surrounded by other people, even if the crowd is starting to get rowdier as evening sets in.

The bar isn't the only thing he can't leave behind. Inside his mind, he keeps replaying memories. His father's death. The devastating fires. Sienna's crying sister. The images loop through his mind endlessly, and he knows going home alone would only make it worse.

"Did you hear about the fires?"

For a moment, Troy thinks he is still buried in his own thoughts. Then, he takes in his surroundings. The bar. The drink in front of him. Gerald is sitting beside him, staring at him with wild eyes.

"Yeah. Saw it on the news."

The television is still playing in the corner of the room, but

Troy has managed to tune it out. There is enough death and destruction in his past; he doesn't need to be consumed with the dangers of the present.

"It's spreading. Bad," Gerald says. "On the east side of the mountain."

Gerald's urgency now makes sense. The flames are headed in the direction of Troy's rental cabins.

"You got any renters this week?"

"All three are full," Troy says, standing without finishing his food.

A wave of déjà vu washes over him. He's been in this situation before, and yet, he wasn't really here. He'd heard about the fire when he was thousands of miles away, defending his country, but he still has the same physical reaction. Twisting stomach, freezing nerves. In that moment, away from his father and the place he'd called home, he'd felt helpless. There was nothing to do.

This time, it is different. This time, if people need him, he can do something to help. A new feeling roots inside of him.

Hope. This time can be different.

He drops a twenty on the table and rushes out the front door.

FORTY-NINE

SIENNA

The blaze is getting stronger.

An uncontrollable inferno devastating everything in its path. The fire is hungry, feasting on an unlimited source of fuel —limp grass, withered leaves, dry bark... it's all devoured, making the blaze stronger with each passing second. From where I stand, I don't understand how anything man-made could ever stop it; the firestorm is that powerful. The wind blows heavily, fanning the flames, making them stronger.

I remember what Troy told me about the previous wildfires in this area. The destruction. The loss of life. The fires are at a distance now but appear to be moving in this direction. If we don't find a way out of here soon, we may lose our chance.

All the lights are on inside the cabin, stinging my eyes as I emerge from the dark outdoors. And yet not so dark, because as I just witnessed, the forest in the distance is alight with fire, uncontrollable and raging. It takes several seconds for my senses to adjust, to wrangle my thoughts into submission.

Help. I need to find help. And I need to get out of here.

Suddenly, I remember my car. It's dark and the roads are windy, but anything is better than staying here. I can drive slowly, maybe make it to the bottom of the mountain and tell someone one of our group is missing. I can tell them about the fires, if they don't already know. Or maybe I could call Troy, when I get a signal. Whatever my plan, every instinct in my body is telling me to escape now, before Colby or any of the others come back.

I rush to the kitchen. On the center island sits the bowl where we'd all put our keys, but the dish is now empty. My keys, and all the others, are missing. Did someone deliberately take them? I know I never put the keys in my bag or room for fear of losing them; taking time to search for them will only waste minutes in a situation where every moment counts.

I race to the front door, ready to take on the burning wilderness, hoping to lay eyes on someone else, anyone else, just so I won't feel so alone, when I hear voices coming from the front porch. My hand is only inches above the doorknob, but I freeze, waiting. Some deep intuition from inside is telling me not to open it, the same feeling I've had countless times this weekend, like someone is just within reach, someone I want to avoid.

"You lied to me." It's Nessa's voice. She sounds frenzied and out of breath. Agitated. "You lied to all of us. And now—"

"Look, I'm trying to protect us," Harper responds, sounding just as tired. "That's all I've tried to do—"

The door swings open, and the duo jumps back at the sight of me. It's clear from their expressions they weren't expecting to see me, or anyone else, but it appears their own adrenaline is pumping too hard for them to realize I overheard them.

"Did you find Matilda?" I ask, my curiosity burning to know what they were talking about.

"No. We've searched all over. Colby is still out there," Harper says. "Where have you been?"

"I came back because..." My thoughts trail away. I'm trying hard to keep up with everything that's happening— Matilda is lost, Nessa and Harper are arguing, the fires. Yes, the fires are what's most important now. "Didn't you see the fires in the distance? It looks out of control. I'm afraid we're all in danger."

"I could smell smoke," Nessa says. "I didn't see the flames until we got closer to the cabin."

"We still have to find Mattie," Harper says, ignoring the potential danger of the fires headed in our direction.

The expression on Nessa's face isn't as confident. She looks like she might be on the verge of tears.

"Are you okay?" I ask her.

"I don't know what to do," she says, her voice low. "I'm really afraid. And we still can't find Mattie."

"We're no help to Mattie if we're in danger, too," I say.

"Matilda is lost in the forest because you had to show up and throw around accusations," Harper spits.

That might be true. Their fragile friendships are falling apart because I kept pushing for answers, and even though there are still more to find, the threat of wildfires in the distance must take precedence.

"You're right," I tell her. "But we can worry about Matilda and Colby later. Right now, we need to find a way into town."

"We'll take the cars," Nessa says, coming alive at the suggestion.

"The keys are gone," I tell her.

"What do you mean they're gone?" Harper asks, angrily.

I nod at the bowl on the counter. "Look. Someone took them. I thought maybe one of you went to get help."

"Maybe Colby did," Nessa says, hopefully.

Harper charges out the front door, and we follow. The air around us has thickened more with smoke, a sickly charcoal taste in my mouth. There's a unified disappointment when we see the vehicles still in the driveway—Jackson's BMW, Colby's SUV and my Mustang. If someone left the mountain, they didn't do so by car.

"No Mattie. No keys," Harper says, a rare desperation attached to each word. "We're screwed."

"We can still get help," I say. "We can follow the gravel road back to town."

"I'm getting a flashlight," Harper says. "I'm not staying out here without something."

Before I can stop her, she's gone back inside. It leaves me only a few minutes alone with Nessa. Maybe I can figure out what's bothering her, because it appears to be something more than Matilda's disappearance or the impending wildfires.

"Nessa, what's wrong?" I ask her.

"It's like Harper said," she begins. "We're all worried about Mattie. And now the fires."

And yet Nessa's version of worried looks very different from Harper's. The former looks afraid, while the latter is on an angry mission.

"I heard the two of you talking before you came inside," I say. "You called Harper a liar."

Nessa shakes her head. "Emotions are running high. I don't know what I'm saying. I got lost in the woods myself. Until I made it back to the house and saw Harper."

I place my hands on her shoulders, an act that seems to calm her. Her body stills ever so slightly.

"I know they're your friends, Nessa. You care about all of them. But it's time to stop keeping secrets. We've already lost my sister because of them. If Harper or anyone else is lying about something, you need to tell me."

Nessa refuses to look at me for several seconds, and when she does, I understand why. Her eyes are beginning to water.

"When you were confronting the rest of us yesterday, you wanted to know—"

Before she can finish her sentence, Harper appears in the doorway. She's holding two flashlights in her hands. Nessa makes a face, one that tells me I'd better change the subject.

"I only found two flashlights. I know there were more when that hillbilly was giving us a tour on the first day."

"Maybe Colby came back and got them," I say. "After Matilda took off."

"Why would he take so many?" Harper says. We watch from the doorway as she goes back inside, pacing back inside to the kitchen, opening and slamming cabinets, searching for something, I'm not even sure she knows what. "I wonder if Colby took the flashlights on purpose."

Could she be right? Is Colby using the chaos and confusion to make a clean break from the rest of us? The thoughts trigger a memory from earlier, when I was alone in the woods.

"I heard a scream," I say. "Before I ran back to the house. Was it either of you?"

Nessa looks at Harper, who has joined us back outside, for only a second, her eyes falling back on the porch. "I heard it, too."

"I'm not sure if I screamed or not," Harper says. She hands me the second flashlight, keeping the other one for herself. "It's terrifying out here in the dark."

Harper's right. The woods are too unknown, too dangerous. Terrifying. But with the wildfires raging in the distance, staying here even a few minutes longer seems a risk we shouldn't take. No matter how frightened we might be of the forest, we must find our way through it if we want to survive. I scan the area from left to right, taking in one more assessment of the place before we take off, and that's when something catches my attention.

The trash box is slightly ajar, the chain holding the lid in place unraveled. I take a step closer.

"I think we'll be safe if we stick together," Harper says. She's still staring out ahead and hasn't seen me walk away. "We should go before we lose more time."

"Just a second," I say, moving closer to the trash box.

"What are you doing?" Nessa asks, only steps behind me. She's watching me, nervously.

"This looks different," I say. "The lid wasn't like this before. There's something in here."

"Who cares?" Harper says. "We need to get away from the cabin."

I ignore her, even if she's right, because something about the trash box in front of me is catching my attention. A feeling inside begging me to look. I reach out my hand slowly, lifting the wooden lid. With my other hand, I raise the small flashlight.

"Sienna, what are you—"

Harper's question is cut short by the sound of my screaming.

It's Matilda.

She's dead, her body stuffed inside the box.

FIFTY

TROY

Troy hangs up the phone, relieved.

His first call was to the family staying at Celebration Springs. They had seen the wildfires on the news and thought it best to evacuate. They're staying in a hotel closer to town along the strip, so they should be safe through the night.

He reached the couple staying at Mountain Serenity just before they were tucking in for the night. They were a little apprehensive when he told them they needed to evacuate because they couldn't see any fires from their balcony, but Troy explained how quickly the fires can take over. He's lucky he caught them before bed, God forbid the flames reach them while they were sleeping. Reluctantly, they accepted his directions to a local church that had opened its doors to evacuees.

His relief quickly faded when he thought about the third cabin, the group that had been bugging him all weekend. He'd tried the house phone three times, but it wouldn't even ring. He wasn't sure how far the fires had spread, but it wouldn't be unusual for the flames to mess with the power lines. Cell phone service is always patchy, and with Jackson in the hospital, he doesn't have any of the other renters' numbers to call.

Troy is sitting behind the wheel of his pickup truck. He slams his feet against the floorboards and curses. What was he to do? He doesn't trust that group to find their way out of a wet paper bag, let alone find safety amid a burning wilderness. But he knows the fire and rescue teams are already overwhelmed. Some homes in the area have already been overtaken by the flames. At least, that's what the news report said fifteen minutes ago. No telling how much more damage has been done since then. Even in the center of town, there's a red-orange hue in the sky, ash falling like snow.

All he knows is that the wildfires are heading towards his rental cabin, and that none of his renters will answer the damn phone.

Cursing again, he opens his car door and exits. He goes around to the bed of the truck, where his dogs are barking with excitement. He helps them both down by the collar and attaches their leashes.

The bell above the glass door dings when he walks inside. Rosie, like all the other workers and patrons, has her eyes glued to the television, assessing the situation for how bad it could get.

"Can you do me a favor?" Troy says, the dogs yelping behind him.

"Oh, goodness. I was worried about you. The fires have gotten so much worse since you left."

"I have to take care of something," Troy says, getting to the point. "Will you keep an eye on my dogs?"

"Troy, what are you doing?" Rosie asks cautiously.

"Just keep an eye on 'em for me. Okay?"

She nods slowly, but the thin line of her lips speaks of displeasure. Before he walks outside, he hears Rosie shout, "Be careful."

He gives her a little wave before getting back inside his truck. Sometimes it sucks being such a good person, Troy thinks. It's what led him to enlist in the military. It's what brought him back to his Podunk town to revive his father's dying dream. And it's what is urging him to take on raging wild-fires in order to save a group of people he doesn't even know.

FIFTY-ONE

SIENNA

Matilda's arms and legs are folded over one another unnaturally, her eyes are open wide, and a trail of blood runs down her left cheek.

I open my mouth and a rattling scream rings out. I've never made a sound like this before, I'm sure of it, and I've never felt this level of fear either. Harper and Nessa react, rushing over to see what I've found, and they begin screaming, too.

"Is she dead?" Nessa cries.

"She has to be," I say, tearing my eyes away, but not daring to lower the lid. I stumble down the steps and retch as soon as my feet hit the hard ground. After several deep gasps, I say, "We have to get out of here."

"What's happening?"

The voice isn't Harper's or Nessa's. I hold out the flashlight, and that's when I see Colby running toward us. Our screams led him straight to us. I raise the flashlight as though it were a weapon.

"Don't come any closer!"

"I heard screaming." Ignoring my warning, he rushes to the front porch. He stops when he sees the raised lid of the trash box, moves closer to peer inside. When he sees, he throws himself against the porch railing, vomiting onto the ground below.

"You killed Mattie!" Nessa screams at Colby, but instead of running to the forest, she retreats to the safety of the house.

I follow her. Harper comes next, slamming the front door shut, but before the lock can latch, something starts pushing from the other side. It's Colby, fighting his way in.

"Leave us alone," Harper yells.

"Not until you tell me what happened," Colby says. He's far stronger than her, and eventually the door swings open, making a loud sound as it hits the adjoining wall. "One of you killed Mattie."

"We didn't kill her," Nessa says. "We couldn't even find her."

"She must have made her way back to the house," Colby says, "and when she did, one of you attacked her."

"We didn't," Harper yells back. "We were out in the woods with you. Searching."

"You couldn't have been together the entire time," he says. "At one point, I ran into Sienna, and she was alone."

"I came back to the cabin after that. Alone." I focus my attention on Nessa. "When Harper and Nessa showed up, they were fighting. You called her a liar. Why?"

Nessa looks to Harper, then at the floor. "It doesn't matter. Nothing matters now," she says weakly. "Mattie is dead."

"Someone in this room did it," Colby says. "It's time everyone starts telling the truth. Did you see something happen to Mattie? Is that why you were fighting with Harper?"

"No!" Harper shouts, defensively. "I keep telling you, none of us saw her!"

"Then what were you fighting about?" I ask Nessa.

"I was asking her why she lied about her alibi. She said she was with me on the night Samantha died, but it's not true. She left at midnight, and never came back."

"I decided to leave early and sleep in my own bed," Harper says. "I didn't want Nessa to say anything because I didn't want to be treated the way you're treating me now. Like I'm a suspect."

"But you did lie," I say, each new blow refueling my rage.

"I'm not the only one," Harper says, looking at Colby. "You weren't out of town with friends that weekend. You were with Mattie at some hotel across town."

"How would you know?"

"I saw pictures on her phone. A week later, we were trying to find pictures for Sammie's memorial service, and I found them. The two of you were so stupid thinking you could get away with your little affair. Sammie could have figured it out, too. Maybe she confronted you about where you'd been that weekend, and that's why you killed her."

"Enough!" Nessa shouts. "We can argue about Sammie and Mattie later. Right now, we need to get off this mountain before the fires—"

The lights in the house cut out, and suddenly we're plunged into an even deeper darkness than the world outside.

FIFTY-TWO

Fear, cold and sharp, climbs my spine. It's one thing to be in the darkness outside, but here, inside the cabin, it feels like there is no escape. I hold out my hand and try to touch Nessa, but the very spot where she stood only moments ago is now empty.

"Nessa?"

"Did someone cut the lights?" It sounds like she's moved across the room. "And what's that smell?"

"It's the fires," I say making my way to her. "They've probably messed with the electricity. We need to stay together."

In her panic and confusion, Nessa refuses to listen. I hear her footsteps as she moves around the living room, bumping into furniture in the darkness. The backdoor slides open, a reflection of moonlight glinting off the glass. I can make out the silhouette of someone standing. Is it Nessa going outside? Or is someone coming in?

"Nessa?" I call out again, but there is no response. Her ragged breaths and worried shuffling have disappeared, and I get the sickening feeling of being alone in the dark house.

I cower, walking back in the direction of the living room. Maybe being alone is better than being out there with them, in the endless dark. I still don't know who I can trust—Nessa, Colby, Harper—one of them had to have killed Matilda. At least. What if they're all in on this together?

Nessa had accused Harper of lying about her alibi when the lights went out. Their loyalty to one another is beginning to fold. I'd say whoever is behind this cut the wires on purpose, but that can't be true. We were all in there together when the house went dark. I fear the wildfires are getting closer.

I grab the flashlight Harper gave me earlier. As I struggle to turn it on, I realize my hands are shaking. When the light appears, I wave the torch around the room, casting a dull, yellow glow, but there is no one else in the room with me. I reach into my pocket and grab my phone, checking for service one more time, but there is nothing.

No keys. No service. Very little light.

The overwhelming danger is becoming more real.

The sliding glass door remains open, the moonlight pouring inside the cabin. Beyond that is the dangerous orange sky. I run to the back balcony, waving the small flashlight from left to right.

"Nessa?" Where could she have gone? If she took off in a panic toward the woods, she could get lost in the wilderness. "Harper?"

No one responds. I follow the length of the balcony and descend the short wooden stairs leading to the ground-level at the side of the house. I'm running around to the front when I hear a sound coming from the opposite direction. Twigs and branches breaking in the woods.

Turning, I stand and wait for whatever might appear, my fingers clenched tightly around the light in my hand.

Something is coming through the foliage. The leaves and branches start shaking heavily. Then, out of the darkness, a person appears.

Harper.

She's panting, holding one hand against her forehead. When she gets closer, I see a smear of blood across her face.

"What happened?" I ask her.

"We need to get out of here. Now."

"What happened?" I repeat.

"It's Colby. He's lost his mind."

"Colby?"

"He attacked me in the woods."

"Why?"

"I don't know. I didn't even know he was near me. We took off in different directions when the lights went out. Next thing I know, he steps out from behind a tree and whacks me over the head with my own flashlight." Her voice gets higher, more fragile. "I think he's the one who killed Mattie."

"What do you mean?"

"She already told the truth about when their relationship started," she says. "She never knew about what happened between Sammie and Roy Balding. Now that she does, she might tell someone, and he had to stop her."

"What about Nessa?"

"I lost sight of her. I followed her outside... then she was just gone. It's too dark to see anything. We need to get out of here," she says. "I'll drive Jackson's car."

"The keys are gone," I remind her. "All the keys are gone."

"Shit. We're stranded."

"We can't leave Nessa anyway, not if you think Colby is likely to hurt her."

"Colby already attacked me once. I'm not going to let him get a second chance," she says, her voice breaking, reaching a pitch I haven't heard since we were middle schoolers, an innocent, fresh fear. "I think you were right about someone hurting Sammie. It must have been him. You were right all along."

"We can't stay here," I decide. "It must be a two-mile walk into town."

"You aren't suggesting—"

"What else can we do? Matilda's dead and Nessa is missing. And you said Colby attacked you. And the fires are getting closer."

Harper brings a hand to her head. She nods slowly. "You're right. If we stay on the path, it can't be that hard, right?"

Harper and I walk around to the front of the house when a sound from the woods stops us in our tracks. It sounds like something loud and heavy is falling.

"Wait," Harper says, holding out her arm. I raise my flashlight, but it's hard to make out anything.

The night forest turns quiet, as though all of nature is on pause, waiting for whatever might come next. That's when I see something dark emerging from the treeline across the driveway. A human. A man.

I lock my arm in place, determined to see who or what is coming in our direction. The weak light makes it hard to see, but he's eventually close enough I can identify him. In one hand, he holds the heavy flashlight Harper had minutes earlier, and there is a stripe of blood across his shirt.

"Oh, Colby," I say to him, weakly. "What did you do?"

FIFTY-THREE

Colby charges the house, but I raise my flashlight, warning him. "Don't get any closer."

He halts, raising both hands. "Listen to me, please. I haven't done anything."

"You did this!" Harper screams at him. "Just like you attacked me in the woods."

"I... I didn't." Colby looks at me. "You have to listen. Mattie —" Colby cuts his eyes to my left, staring at the box in horror. "Sienna, we have to get out of here."

"I'm not going anywhere with you!"

"You don't understand," he says, coming closer. "I didn't kill Mattie. I didn't do any of this. It's Harper."

"What?" Harper is to my right.

"I saw her in the woods," Colby says. "She was chasing Mattie."

"I wasn't," Harper says. "He's lying."

"She's behind all of this, I swear," Colby says. "She loosened the panels so that Jackson would fall. She killed Mattie. Who knows what happened to Nessa?"

I haven't seen Nessa since the lights went out. I look

between the two of them, not knowing who to believe. Nessa accused Harper of lying about her whereabouts, but Colby is the one who locked me in a bedroom. I'm not sure I know what either of them is capable of.

"We'll walk down the mountain however long it takes to get service, then we'll call the police. They can sort it out," I say, taking a cautious step forward.

"Sienna!"

Colby screams my name and begins charging. I dodge to avoid him, when I see another threat to my right. Harper has just lunged at me. I barely get out of the way in time for Colby to tackle her, and they both fall hard against the front porch.

"Harper?" I struggle to get to my feet, out of breath. "What are you doing?"

The weak light shines in the dark, illuminating the fight between Colby and Harper on the ground. Harper wriggles out from beneath him, the heavy flashlight now in her grasp, and with one confident swoop, she brings the heavy metal down hard on the top of his head.

I bring a hand to my mouth to stifle my scream. Now on my feet, I begin shuffling backwards, trying to get away. Harper stands, staring at me with a murderous glare. "Sienna, you need to listen to me."

I take off running, immediately shutting off the flashlight to better conceal my whereabouts. I climb down the same hill I had to cross when trying to help Jackson, but it's much harder in the darkness. Branches bite at my arms and ankles as I try, desperately, to get away.

"Sienna?"

Harper calls out to me, but there's distance between us.

"We can't go to the police about any of this. Do you understand that now?"

I'm afraid the sound of my running will draw more attention. Passing a large tree, I duck down, hiding against its trunk, and listen to the sounds of Harper coming closer.

"You know me," Harper continues, her voice getting louder. "None of it was ever supposed to happen like this. All I was trying to do was protect everyone, and things just snowballed.

"We all tried talking to Samantha, but it wasn't enough. She was adamant about going to the police over Balding. She refused to see how that would tank the company. I showed up at her condo that night to try and talk her out of it. I thought she might listen to me, her oldest friend.

"Instead, she lashed out. She accused me of being insincere. She said I was happy about what had happened to her, because it put the power dynamics in my favor. Can you believe that? My best friend, or so I thought. Then, she said Colby was cheating and accused him of doing it with me. It wasn't true, any of it, but she wouldn't listen.

"Somehow, we ended up on the balcony. She was struggling to get away from me, and I grabbed her arm. I didn't mean to put her off balance. I didn't mean to push her. It was an accident, do you understand?"

Warm tears fall down my cheeks, making the hand over my mouth slippery. I continue breathing through my nose, trying not to react and give away my location.

"And no one needed to know. No one even questioned what happened, until you showed up and started causing trouble."

A hard thud hits the tree above my head, bark falling into my hair. I move out of the way, quickly, but Harper knows where I am now. I keep trying to put distance between us, but it's hard to move through the heavy foliage. Harper is also struggling.

"It was an accident," Harper continues. "I loved her, too."

"You left her there," I say. "If you had gotten her help, she might have survived. But you just left her. And what about what Colby was saying? Did you really try to hurt Jackson?"

"The two of you were conspiring against me. I heard you talking. I just wanted to shut him up."

"What about Matilda? And Nessa?"

"Matilda can't keep her mouth shut. She would have told the police about Sammie and Balding. Then all of this would have been for nothing."

She swings the flashlight again, but there's still enough distance between us, it doesn't land. Realizing I only have a small amount of time left before she catches up to me, I use the only weapon I have, the small flashlight. I throw it hard and, miraculously, it hits Harper square in the face. She yelps out in pain.

Momentarily stunned, I use the opportunity to run up the hill. I hear Harper coming after me, but there's enough of a gap now, I might be able to get away. I'm coming up toward the left side of the house, when I trip over something, falling hard on my chest. I feel the ground, trying to find my balance, when my hand touches something warm and fleshy. I move closer, trying to see in the darkness.

It's Nessa, lying on the ground beside the house.

Unable to stop myself, I scream, hurrying to my feet. I jump forward, trying desperately to get back to even ground. If I can make it to the main road before Harper, at least I'll have a chance. I can run for my life.

But the fires are closer now, quickly consuming the foliage where Harper and I were just arguing. They're so close now, I can feel the heat of the flames.

Sparks bounce off the sides of trees, reminding me of the sparklers Samantha and I would wave around like wands on the Fourth of July, trying to spell out our names in the air before the magic ran out, but there's nothing nostalgic or magical about these fiery specs. They're nothing more than a warning of what's to come. A wall of fire, edging ever closer.

I believed nightfall was to be feared. But darkness is clean and crisp compared to this. A thick, itchy wall of smoke makes it difficult to see, making it increasingly harder to breathe. Maybe the grounds would be easier to navigate during daylight. Then again, if I could see everything that was happening, the mighty forest falling at my feet, that might be more terrifying. The unknown can be a kindness. I'm used to traversing the unknown on my own. In many ways, it's what I've been doing since Samantha's death, pushing forward, relying only on a sense of self-reliance to get me through to the other side.

I've found what I came here for: answers about Samantha's death. It could still all be in vain if I perish here on this mountain alongside the same people who betrayed her.

I finally make it up the embankment, coming around the left side of the house. Colby is still lying on the front porch, motionless.

I try to remain calm. I inhale deeply, fully aware that my clean air supply could soon be limited. I'm grateful for each breath, hoping it will give me the peace of mind I need to move forward. It's terrifying when I have two threats at my back: wildfires in the distance, and Harper somewhere closer.

The wind blows past me, my hair flying backwards in the direction of the flames. I march forward, but I can't ignore the weakness taking over my body. Smoke must already be filling my lungs. My adrenaline makes my heart pump faster, and I'm not sure how much longer my body can power through.

I scoot up close to the house and hunker down, hoping if the flames and smoke persist, it will at least go around me, that maybe the house will be a barrier between me and death. I take off my jacket and hold it over my head, as though the fabric will be a deterrent. My mouth hovers only inches above the ground. I breathe deeply. The air near the soil feels cleaner there, but like every other assurance in this situation, I know it's only temporary.

I had feared the flames. Hot, orange bursts biting at my skin, leaving everything in its wake mere ashes. Now, it's the smoke I fear. I imagine the dangerous mist diving deeper and deeper, filling my lungs and scratching my throat, until there's nothing left.

I'd thought death might be accompanied with a sense of peace, an understanding. But this—the merciless smoke and approaching heat, leaves me in a state of confusion that's more terrifying than anything I've ever experienced before. I don't know if I will find my way. Until...

Lights, bright and blinding. Two gracious orbs cutting through the smoke, create a clearing.

Someone is here.

FIFTY-FOUR

TROY

Troy is grateful none of the roads leading toward Sunset Memories are blocked. Even though people have already been urged to evacuate that side of the mountain, he knows enough back roads to make it to his destination without being stopped.

He is even more relieved not to pass any fires along his trek up the mountain, although he can see flames in the distance, and the pungent smoke is getting so thick, it is starting to sneak inside his truck.

When he pulls into the clearing, his stomach sinks at the sight of all the cars, the darkness inside the house, and the bruised orange and red sky above. Do any of them even know what is happening? Or worse, have they been on a hike and are lost out there in the burning wilderness?

Then, something darts in front of his headlights. A figure. Sienna, the girl he'd driven to the hospital the day before.

"Help!" she shouts, running toward the car.

"Where is everyone?" Troy asks when he steps out of his truck.

"We need to leave. Now."

Without hesitation, Sienna hops into the truck, slamming the door behind her.

"I need to know where everyone is," Troy says. "Wildfires are moving in this direction. This might be our last chance—"

Something hard and loud hits his windshield. The sound makes him jump. That's when he sees another girl coming around the corner of the car.

"Leave her. We have to go!" Sienna shouts.

"Why?" Troy asks, just as another hit strikes his car, this time the passenger side window. It's the blonde girl, he realizes. She's hitting his truck with something, trying to get inside.

"She killed my sister," Sienna says, tears starting to flow. "We have to go. Now."

Troy reaches forward, grabbing the pistol he always carries in the glove compartment of his car. In the darkness, the blonde girl sees the weapon, and bolts in the opposite direction, disappearing into the forest.

"What the hell is going on?"

"I already told you. Harper killed my sister. And Mattie."

"Is that Harper?"

"Yes."

"She's running toward the woods. She won't make it out."

"I don't care!"

It's not in Troy's nature to leave someone behind, but if what Sienna is saying is true, then they're in more danger staying here. Reluctantly, he puts the truck in reverse, and backs out onto the main road.

A loud scream cuts through the night before they take off.

"Wait!" calls the voice. "Please, help!"

Troy looks back to the house. That's when he sees two people limping toward his truck. When they get closer, he can see they are both bleeding from the head.

"Colby?" Sienna asks, bewildered. "Nessa?"

She opens her door. Quickly, Troy moves around and helps the wounded people into his truck.

"What happened?" the girl asks, a shaky hand on her bleeding head.

"It was Harper," Sienna says. "All of it was Harper."

Troy doesn't know what she means, and he's not sure he wants to know.

All he cares about is getting himself and the rest of the group to safety.

FIFTY-FIVE

SIENNA

Cold, clean air pumps into the plastic oxygen mask. I gulp each breath, thankfully. Even though I felt fine, I wasn't going to take any chances. I've seen *This Is Us*.

"You're lucky," a nurse says. She is standing in front of Sienna, writing down her vitals. "The whole town was lucky. Not like last time. Last I heard, firefighters had the burn under control."

I smile. On the surface, it doesn't seem I have much to celebrate. Samantha is still dead, and thanks to this weekend, I finally know who killed her. Harper, her oldest friend. There's so much sadness wrapped up in that, and yet there's relief in knowing the truth has finally come out.

After breathing deeply for several more seconds, I ask the nurse, "How's my friend?"

"The one who brought you? He's fine. I think he's resting in a room down the hall. This whole floor is devoted to people escaping the wildfires."

"I'll let him rest," I say, putting the mask back to my face. I pull it away again. "I do have another friend here."

The nurse gives me directions to Jackson's room. Even

though it's only been a few hours since I was last here, I'd get lost if I tried to find it on my own. The hospital hallways are much like the wilderness; everything looks the same.

I'm worried he'll be asleep, given how late it is, but I can hear his television blaring before I turn the corner. He's propped up in bed, watching rerun episodes of *Jersey Shore*.

"Thank God," he says when he sees me. He throws back his head, in relief. "I tried calling you like a million times. I was scared shitless when I heard they were evacuating cabins on the mountain."

"You know service was shit," I say, sitting in the navy chair by his bed. "And a lot has happened since I left."

Jackson would have thought we'd spent the past several hours battling wildfires, like everyone else in the area. He had no idea our situation was much more dangerous. I fill him in on everything that's happened since I ended our last phone call. Finding the missing pages and learning Samantha's devastating secret. Confronting the others, which led to everyone darting off in different directions. Harper's confession, not only to pushing Samantha, but to also murdering Matilda and trying to hurt the others, too.

When I finish telling the story, he's left speechless. Tears are building in the corners of his eyes, and it's hard to tell if he wants to scream or sob.

"You never should have gone back there."

"We would never have learned the truth if I hadn't."

"At least there's that." He pauses. "And Matilda?"

"I know. It's heartbreaking. Even if she did betray Samantha, she didn't deserve that. None of us did. But if Harper had gotten her way, I believe she would have killed all of us to keep her secrets safe."

"Did the police arrest her?"

"They will, if they can find her. Last I saw her, she went running into the woods, in the direction of the fires." I pause, considering the possible outcomes. "Who knows if she'll ever make it off the mountain."

"After what she did to Sammie and Mattie, I'm not sure she deserves to be saved." He looks away. "You were right from the very beginning. I can't believe all of them knew what happened to her and never did anything about it."

"You were right, too. They were keeping the assault a secret from you. And Matilda. They must have known you wouldn't keep quiet."

"I've spent the bulk of the last decade with those people. And none of them were my real friends to begin with."

"Samantha was your friend," I tell him. "She cared about you more than you know."

"Yeah." His voice breaks. "I cared about her, too."

Another pause, both of us thinking. My mind continues to replay the past couple of hours. I sense Jackson's mind is traveling further back, to simpler times when my sister was still alive and everyone's betrayals weren't out in the open. He must feel so helpless, sitting there being fed information, unable to do anything about it.

"There was something else in the journal about you," I begin. "Something I didn't tell you about."

"What?"

"Samantha had feelings for you, too. She wanted to remain loyal to Colby, and I think her head was all over the place in the months leading up to her death, trying to figure out which of her friends she could trust. But she did care about you, Jackson. I thought you should know that."

Now, Jackson doesn't try to remain stoic. He begins to cry. When he composes himself, he says, "Thank you for telling me. It helps to know she knew I was really in her corner, especially considering how the others betrayed her."

"We were both there for her," I say, reaching for his hand. "I just wish we could have been there when she needed us most."

Silence again, as we each trail away into our thoughts. There's so much both of us would change, for Samantha, for us, but it feels like this weekend finally brought her justice, which is the most we can do for her now.

"The journal," Jackson says.

"What about it?"

"Did you ever find it?"

"No. I'm convinced the others did something with it. I guess we'll never know."

Jackson nods. "Like you said, it's a long road ahead. At least we don't have to feel like we're traveling it alone."

I squeeze his hand a little tighter as he leans back onto the bed. He uses the remote to turn up the volume, and we stop talking. The next hour, we remain silent, listening to guidos and guidettes arguing about nonsense.

FIFTY-SIX

Earlier That Day

Four people hiked along the dirt trail, then kept going long after the trail ended, and all that was left was fallen leaves and broken branches.

"We've gone far enough," Nessa said. She smacked at her exposed skin, unable to shake the feeling that mosquitos and other bugs were nibbling.

"Just a little further," Harper said, determined.

"You don't even know where you're going," Matilda said. She wasn't used to breaking a sweat, and the steep incline of their trek had left her winded.

"We need to be far away from the cabin," Harper said.

"It's not like she's going to come after us," Nessa said.

"We should keep going," Harper said.

"I'm done." Matilda stood defiantly with her hands on her hips. "Colby, are you with me?"

The only man in the group barely paid any attention to the women. All of his attention was devoted to the journal in his hands. He hadn't stopped reading since they left the cabin.

He'd be willing to hike forever, as long as it meant he could continue to gather information.

"Give it here," Harper snapped, backtracking to where Colby stood. She snatched it out of his hands, impatiently.

"I'm still reading—"

"We already know what's in there. Sienna told us everything."

"I wanted to see it for myself," he said. "Make sure she didn't say anything about that night."

"What night?" Matilda asked, still struggling to breathe normally.

"Nothing," Colby said quickly. "You're right. We already know the horrible things she said about us. Now what?"

"We need to get rid of it," Harper said.

"That's what we came here to do," Nessa said, irritated. "Just leave it and let's head back."

"No!" Matilda was almost hysterical. "If we leave it, we run the risk of someone finding it."

"We're in the middle of nowhere," Nessa said. "Even if Sienna wanted to find it, she wouldn't know where to look."

"And what if someone else finds it? A camper or a hiker? I'm not leaving written proof of all of Samantha's grievances."

"What are you suggesting?" Colby asked.

Harper reached into her pocket and retrieved Jackson's lighter. "We'll burn it."

"Fine. Whatever." Nessa was beyond checked out. "Just hurry so we can get back."

Harper flipped through the pages, but unlike Colby, she didn't take the time to read them. The familiar handwriting meant nothing to her. All that mattered was keeping her secrets from the rest of the world. She held the open journal in one hand, flicked the lighter with her other.

"Be careful," Matilda warned. "You're going to burn yourself."

Harper wasn't listening. Her eyes were fixed on the burning pages. She watched with titillating amusement as the flames danced.

"What's that?" Nessa asked, looking further into the woods. She heard something, a small sound. But the images in her mind —hunters, mountain lions, bears—were growing much larger, fear taking over.

"It's nothing," Colby said.

"I heard it, too," Matilda said, her eyes wide yet not knowing where to look.

"I'm leaving," Nessa announced.

"Me too." Matilda followed her.

"What about the journal?" Colby asked.

"Leave it. It's damaged enough."

"Harper?" Colby called out. Finally, she looked up. "We're heading back."

"Yeah. Yeah. I'm coming."

She threw the burning journal on the ground and stomped it with the heel of her boot, until almost all the fire was extinguished. Satisfied, she hiked back toward the trail, confident her secrets were safe at last.

But the flames didn't go out. The broken twigs and fallen leaves on the ground served as the perfect kindling, the increasing winds the perfect accelerator. Without a drop of rain in sight, the journal burned hotter and faster.

The group didn't know it, as they marched back to where they'd come from, but in their absence, they'd left something dangerous, in the same way one small act can lead to the destruction of so much more.

FIFTY-SEVEN

SIENNA

Three Months Later

Gone are the colorful leaves and lush greenery. They've fallen away, hidden beneath lumps of melting snow on the ground.

More flakes fall from the sky, and it makes me wonder what the place will look like come morning.

If you'd told me on the night of my rescue that I'd be returning to the scene of my near death, I would have called you a liar.

But a lot can change in three months. Just ask Harper.

Despite Troy's concern, she did make her way off the mountain that night. It didn't take the police long to arrest her after I gave them my statement at the hospital. She went from being the smiling poster child of Sunshine Aesthetics to living in an eight-by-eight cell, receiving only one hour of outside time a day. This time of year, I'd say even that one hour is nothing but rainy and gray. I can't help but smile at the irony.

As much as I wish she was out of my life completely, that's not the case. They've just started to try her for Samantha and Matilda's murders. She's yet to put in a plea, but I'm hoping, given the evidence stacked against her, she'll make it easier for all of us by avoiding a trial.

The last thing I want is to relive the events at the cabin in front of a jury box, but I'm willing to do it, if that's what it takes.

At least this time, I don't feel like I'm going up against my sister's killer alone. There's Jackson, too. He is as resolute as I am about getting justice. Now that Sunshine Aesthetics is tied down with multiple lawsuits, he's found a job with a different firm. He's been quite successful. A natural charmer, and now sober, I believe he has the potential to do great things in the world. Samantha always thought him capable.

Nessa has moved on, too. Across the country, actually. She's headlining a start-up based in California. I hope Silicon Valley can handle the likes of her. I'm not sure I'll ever be able to forgive her for the way she treated Samantha. Colby is equally hard to forgive for his lying and gaslighting, however, he's the one suffering the most for his actions. He's now lost two girl-friends and if that can't teach you something about character, I don't know what will.

Thankfully, Roy Balding didn't walk away unscathed either. I reported the incident with my sister to the authorities, although the letter she'd written was lost during the struggle to escape the cabin. Unfortunately, when you don't have someone to testify, little can be done. But the allegations made the papers, and after that, several other women came forward. People he'd worked with, clients, even his assistant. He may not serve a day for what he did to Samantha, but I rest easy knowing he's been charged for his other crimes and won't have the opportunity to hurt another woman ever again.

The happiest revelation in recent months is that my parents finally decided to sell Roth Family Cleaners. They were overwhelmed by what happened to me at that cabin and everything that followed. I think it reminded them that even though they lost one child, there was still another one here.

Learning the truth about Samantha's death relieved another burden. Like me, they knew something wasn't right, but didn't know how to vocalize it. Dad stuck to work, and Ma stuck to booze. Learning the truth about what happened, even the heart-breaking parts, has delivered them a little bit of closure.

They've decided to start living their lives instead of drowning in their grief. They're using the profits from the sale to take an extended cruise for the holidays. They were hesitant to leave me behind at first, but I encouraged them to go, believing they might return a more whole version of themselves.

My car slips against the icy roadways as it climbs the mountain. Thankfully, Mountain Serenity isn't as far into the wilderness as the one we visited this fall.

When I pull into the clearing, I see a small, quaint wooden cabin, gray smoke puffing from the chimney. Piles of snow cover the roof and porch steps. It looks like something off a Christmas postcard.

The front door opens, and Troy comes outside. He waves, Twister and Jennings at his feet.

"Thank God," I say when I get out of the car, careful not to slip as I walk toward the porch. "I didn't think my car could make it much farther."

"You got here just in time. They're calling for another three inches during the night. But don't worry. My truck can make it through anything."

We hug awkwardly. Troy and I have been in near constant communication since the night of the wildfires, but this is the first time we've seen each other in person. It started with a phone call from him, to make sure I was okay. Then a few nights later, after I'd had a nightmare, I reached out to him, thinking he was the only person who could really understand.

Phone calls every other night turned into nightly FaceTime calls, and eventually frequent messages throughout the day. When I told him my parents' plans for Christmas, he invited me to one of his cabins—obviously not Sunset Memories. He's actually in the process of selling it.

"My father and I had this tradition at Christmas," he says, helping me with my bags. "He'd block off one of the cabins for the holiday week so we could enjoy it together. It's cozy, but it gets lonely by myself. I'm happy you're here."

"I'm happy, too." My words sound much more sincere than they were last time I was here.

I'm not sure exactly what's building between Troy and me. Maybe a friendship. Maybe more. But I think we're both used to being on our own, and it's nice to feel that solitude slip away, if only for the weekend.

"There are two bedrooms," he says, ever the gentleman. "Let me show you yours."

I unload my belongings in the small room at the back of the house while he prepares the grill for dinner. From my duffel bag, I take the photograph of Samantha and me, now in a new frame, and place it on the bedside table. Next to it, I put my own journal. I've found it helpful to recount my thoughts and feelings the past few months, yet another way Samantha is helping me.

I keep my place with two pages from her journal; it's an entry I decided to keep for myself, before I committed to going to the cabin in the first place. I'm glad I ripped these pages out, otherwise they would be lost with the rest of the journal.

She wrote it last August, on our birthday. It's my favorite entry, and whenever I'm missing her, seeing her handwriting and hearing her voice in my head helps calm me.

I unfold the pages and begin to read.

FIFTY-EIGHT

SAMANTHA'S DIARY

August 2022

Today is my sister's birthday. Okay, so that means it's my birthday, too. As though I haven't been reminded a half dozen times. My phone was filled with messages when I woke up. I received flowers from Colby and my sorority sisters and even a few key investors at the company. The girls have planned an elaborate birthday dinner downtown which I'm sure will lead to drinks and dancing at places I'm too old to visit anymore.

Enough about me. I want to focus on my sister, because I realized when I was scrolling through messages and texts from people I hardly know, I'm missing her more today than normal.

We spoke yesterday for about ten minutes. She was in Paris, getting ready to take the train to some little city I've never heard about and can hardly pronounce. She wanted to check in early because reception can be spotty in the countryside.

Not that I know from experience. Sometimes, I think about starting my life over. Instead of carving out my own path, I dream about following Sienna's lead. She's always so self-deprecating, referring to herself as a failure, but I don't see her that way.

My big sister (by four minutes) is the bravest person I've ever met. From the time she was a girl, she took what other people had to tell her as optional, convinced she knew what was best for her. And she's right. I'm surrounded by people all day—in the office, at events, on social media—and not one of them is as genuine and real as Sienna.

She doesn't care about what is expected of her. She doesn't care about stability. She truly doesn't give two shits about what people think (can you imagine!). I might be the golden child, but she's the one who truly shines, and sometimes I think the person most reluctant to see it is her.

She seeks adventure and finds it. Sure, there have been times I wanted to bring her back, but that was just me being selfish. I realize I'm too set in my ways to ever be as free as her, and sometimes I think we'd be closer if she was a little more grounded, like me.

But she's not like me or anyone else. That's her special type of magic.

Sienna, wherever you are in this big, beautiful world, happy birthday. I love you. I miss you. And I'll always be here waiting, because my life is never complete without you.

A LETTER FROM MIRANDA

Dear Reader,

Thank you for taking the time to read *The Weekend Away*. If you liked it and want information about upcoming releases, sign up with the following link. Your email address will never be shared and you can unsubscribe at any time.

www.bookouture.com/miranda-smith

Although this is a fictional story with a nameless setting, the presence of wildfires was largely influenced by the 2016 wildfires that swept out of the Great Smoky Mountains National Park and into Gatlinburg and Sevier County. More than 17,000 acres were burned, causing hundreds of millions in damage. Most tragically, fourteen lives were lost, and several more people were injured.

Amidst the devastation, I was amazed to see how the community pulled together to help one another. Locals found shelter and provided food and clothing for evacuees. My former place of employment, Cosby High School, opened its doors for those in need. Even country music legend and angel on earth, Dolly Parton, an East Tennessee native, donated millions to support the families that were impacted. The area's sense of community and volunteerism was inspiring, and I tried to represent this sentiment, particularly through the character of Troy.

If you'd like to discuss any of my books, I'd love to connect!

You can find me on social media or get in touch through my website. If you enjoyed *The Weekend Away* I'd appreciate it if you left a review on Amazon. It only takes a few minutes and does wonders in helping readers discover my books for the first time.

Thank you again for your support!

Sincerely,

Miranda Smith

facebook.com/MirandaSmithAuthor

twitter.com/msmithbooks

instagram.com/mirandasmithbooks

ACKNOWLEDGMENTS

Thank you to the people at Bookouture for all their hard work publishing and promoting my books, especially Sarah Hardy, Kim Nash, Jane Eastgate and Liz Hurst. Thank you to my editor, Ruth Tross, for all your input and support. Your insight makes each book the best it can be!

Thank you to the readers, book bloggers, and reviewers for sharing about my books. Without you, this career would not be possible. Each positive review and creative photograph means more to me than you'll ever know.

I'd like to thank my family, which includes my parents, husband, in-laws and extended family. Your encouragement and willingness to help promote my books mean everything to me. To Harrison, Lucy and Christopher, I love you very much.

The driving force of this book is Sienna's love for her sister. I've been blessed with three sisters of my own. This book is dedicated to my youngest sister, Allison, who, as I write this, is likely feeding and cuddling her newborn daughter. The strength you've shown these past several weeks has been inspiring—and you still make it a priority to support whatever I'm doing. Thank you.